THE CLUE OF THE TAPPING HEELS

CHALLENGING questions confront Nancy Drew when she attempts to solve the mystery of the strange tapping sounds in the house of a retired actress. Who is the tapper? How does he gain access to Miss Carter's house, despite securely locked doors and windows? Why do the tapping sounds come in Morse code? Is there a sinister motive behind the prowler's actions?

While trying to learn the answers to these and other puzzling questions, Nancy finds her investigations complicated by the dishonest administrator of a will and by a thief who steals the actress's prize Persian cats.

How Nancy communicates with the ghostlike intruder by tap dancing in code, how she outwits three criminals wanted by the police, and how she brings happiness to Miss Carter in a romantic reunion with the actress's former leading man will thrill the lively young detective's host of fans.

Hopefully Nancy banged on the trap door

NANCY DREW MYSTERY STORIES

The Clue of the Tapping Heels

BY CAROLYN KEENE

PUBLISHERS *Grosset & Dunlap* NEW YORK

PUBLISHED SIMULTANEOUSLY IN CANADA

LIBRARY OF CONGRESS CATALOG CARD
NUMBER: 71-86679
ISBN: 0-448-09516-5 (TRADE EDITION)
ISBN: 0-448-19516-X (LIBRARY EDITION)

PRINTED IN THE UNITED STATES OF AMERICA

Contents

The Clue of the Tapping Heels

CHAPTER I

Tap Code

TAP! TAP! TAP!

"Nancy," said blond, pretty Bess Marvin, "that doesn't sound like a regular tap dance."

"It certainly doesn't," added George Fayne, a dark-haired, athletic girl, who was Bess's cousin. "I could almost imagine it's a code."

"And you'd be right," Nancy Drew replied with a broad grin.

The slender, titian-haired tap dancer stood in the center of the Drews' basement recreation room. Her audience, besides Bess and George, was Mrs. Hannah Gruen, the kindly housekeeper. She had helped to rear Nancy since the death of Mrs. Drew when Nancy was three years old.

Mrs. Gruen said, "Nancy, why don't you tell the girls about your new mystery? After all they've been invited to help solve it."

"Another mystery?" Bess spoke up. "What's this one?"

"It involves a strange tapper," Nancy replied as she dropped into a chair. "Hannah has a friend named Mrs. Bealing. She's a practical nurse. Recently she was called on a case over in Berryville to take care of a Miss Carter who broke her leg."

"What does this have to do with tapping?" George interjected.

Hannah Gruen answered. "Mrs. Bealing is fed up with what's going on at Miss Carter's house. The woman lives alone and breeds Persian cats to sell. My friend didn't bargain on feeding and taking care of a lot of cats. Now, to add to that, she has heard mysterious tapping sounds in the walls at night."

"Ghosts?" George remarked.

"That's what we're supposed to find out," Nancy replied. "Mrs. Bealing says the sounds are like tap dancing. The poor woman hasn't had any time off and very little sleep. Miss Carter wants you and Bess and me to come out to relieve her and solve the mystery."

"It sounds spooky," said Bess, "and I don't know a thing about taking care of Persian cats."

"Cats are cats," Mrs. Gruen stated.

"Well," said Nancy, "would you girls like to go? Miss Carter wants us to visit her until we solve the mystery. You know, I'm to be in the

Rivers Club play that's being given for charity. We're having rehearsals pretty often. I wouldn't be able to stay in Berryville every night, but I could commute."

Bess and George were eager to track down the tapper and said they would ask their parents' permission.

While Bess was telephoning upstairs, George said to Nancy, "You still haven't explained about the code tapping you were doing."

Nancy laughed. "Recently I decided to study Morse code. I thought it would be fun to tap out messages with my heels."

In a few moments Bess was back, smiling. "It's all right for me to go. When do we start?"

"As soon as we can pack a few clothes," Nancy answered.

After George had phoned her mother and was given a green light to work on the mystery, Nancy said she would pick the girls up at their homes in an hour. She telephoned her father at his law office to tell him of the plans.

"So you couldn't resist the challenge of another mystery?" He laughed. "Best of luck, dear, and let me know if you need any help."

Nancy and her father had always been very close and at times he asked her advice on some of his cases. On other occasions, like this one, a mystery had come to her directly.

Berryville, a small suburban community not

far from River Heights where Nancy lived, was filled with cars and shoppers.

"Miss Carter's home is about half a mile from Main Street," Nancy said. "Girls, watch for Amity Place."

A minute later they saw the sign and turned down the tree-shaded street. Flowers bloomed in every yard.

"Look for number thirty-two," Nancy requested.

They had almost reached it when without warning she slammed on the brakes. Bess and George swung forward on the front seat of the convertible.

"What—?" Bess began.

Then she saw why Nancy had stopped so abruptly. An exquisite Persian kitten was wobbling slowly across the road!

"Oh!" Bess cried out. "I'm glad you didn't hit the poor thing. Isn't it darling?"

"I wonder if it belongs to Miss Carter," Nancy replied. "In any case I think we'd better pick up the kitten and take it to her."

She parked the car at the curb and jumped out. As Nancy cuddled the tiny animal, it seemed content and fell asleep at once.

"It's precious!" Bess exclaimed, stroking the titian ball of fluff.

The three girls went up the front walk and

rang the bell of the colonial brick house. A plump, white-haired woman opened the door.

"Hello, Mrs. Bealing," said Nancy and introduced her friends.

"I'm so glad you came," the nurse said. "Things are so spooky around this place. Why, where did you get that kitten, Nancy?"

When she heard that it had been found in the roadway, Mrs. Bealing declared the little creature must be one of Miss Carter's valuable cats. "We'll carry it upstairs and ask her."

The house had a center hallway with wide doorways to adjoining rooms. The furnishings were a pleasant conglomerate of antique and modern pieces. Draperies and fiberglass curtains hung at each window.

Miss Carter sat in a cheerful, sunny bedroom. She was slight in build with gray hair and bright, laughing brown eyes. She welcomed the girls cordially with both hands from a couch. Her right leg was in a cast. A wheel chair stood nearby.

"You were so good to come," she said, and added with a trilly little laugh, "Oh, have you brought me a kitten?"

Nancy shook her head and explained where she had found the animal. "I thought perhaps it belongs to you."

Miss Carter took the kitten on her lap. "Why, I believe this is one of mine," she said quickly.

"But how in the world did it get out of the locked garage and caged area where I keep my pets?"

Though she had not been downstairs in weeks, Miss Carter insisted upon going out to her back yard to investigate. Nancy and George carried the frail woman to the first floor, and Bess brought the wheel chair downstairs.

The first floor was on ground level so there was no difficulty in wheeling Miss Carter across the rear lawn toward the garage. On the way she explained that after purchasing the house she had had no money left to build a cattery for the Persians.

"But my pets seem to be content to sleep on hay on the floor of the garage or up on shelves around the walls. A friend gave me several Persians and thought I might breed them. They do sell for good prices."

By this time they had reached the garage. The big double front doors were locked as well as the entrance door on the right side.

Attached to the left wall of the building was a large cage stretching parallel to the lawn. Several beautiful reddish-haired Persians were strolling about inside.

"They're gorgeous!" Bess burst out.

Miss Carter smiled. "My pets like to sun themselves. They come out of the garage through a doorway that leads into the cage."

Mrs. Bealing handed Nancy the key to the side

door. "Open it carefully," she warned, "so none of the cats can get out."

They all went inside. At once several red Persians leaped outside to the wire enclosure.

"They're really not unfriendly," Miss Carter explained, "just wary of strangers." She began to count her pets.

There was silence for a couple of minutes, then she announced, "Five of them have been stolen!"

"How dreadful!" Nancy exclaimed. "Miss Carter, does that count include the kitten we found on the road?"

"No, that makes one more. Let me see the kitten again."

Mrs. Bealing handed it over. The little Persian was still sound asleep and to everyone's horror did not respond to its mistress's cajoling to wake up.

"This kitten acts as if it has been drugged," Miss Carter said. "Nancy, what do you think?"

Although Nancy had demonstrated her powers as an amateur detective upon many occasions, she had never been asked so soon after accepting a case for an explanation to yet another mystery. Nevertheless, she hazarded a guess.

"Perhaps the thief who took the five larger cats tried to take the kitten also and drugged them all. The man must have dropped this little fellow."

"Then that means the thief wasn't here very

long ago," Miss Carter remarked. "Otherwise the kitten would have gone farther away." The others agreed.

Nancy offered to telephone the police and within ten minutes Detective Keely arrived. He and the girls looked for clues to the thief but found none.

"That kitten does act as if it has been drugged," the officer said. "Suppose I take it along and have a veterinarian examine the little fellow."

After Keely had gone, Miss Carter was taken into the house and Mrs. Bealing started preparations for supper. While waiting, Miss Carter told the girls a little about Persian cats.

"In this country most of the so-called Persians are a crossbreed of Persian and Angora. However, the cats resemble their Persian ancestors more than they do the Angora. You probably noticed that my cats have short, compact bodies and a ruff around their necks."

Bess nodded and giggled. "And I love their little round heads, stubby noses, small ears and bushy tails."

During supper Miss Carter said she was worried that the thief might return for more of her cats.

"Suppose I sleep in the garage," George offered. "I don't mind a bit, and nothing would please me more than to catch that thief!"

Bess spoke up. "I'm not going to let you stay

"Five cats have been stolen!" Miss Carter announced

out there alone. If you sleep in the garage, I will too."

"You won't mind if I don't join you?" Nancy asked. "I'd better stay in the house and try to catch the tapper."

"Good idea," said George. Later she and Bess carried cots and bedding to the garage and the two girls took up their vigil. Miss Carter had already been put to bed. Mrs. Bealing had said good night to the others and gone to her room.

Nancy remained on the first floor. She was too excited to sleep and wondered if the tapper would make a visit to the house that night.

"I think I'll stay right here in the living room and listen for a while," she decided.

One by one Nancy put out the lights, turned off the TV, and curled up in a big chair to wait. Half an hour went by. Nancy finally became drowsy. She was about ready to give up her watch when she suddenly was aroused by tapping sounds. They seemed to be coming from directly beneath her feet!

Nancy's pulse started to race. Was the mysterious tapper in the basement?

CHAPTER II

Animal Uproar

NANCY sat tense, her mind in a quandary. Should she investigate the basement at once?

"I'd better not go alone," Nancy thought. She was tempted to awaken Mrs. Bealing to accompany her but decided against disturbing her.

Nancy had noticed that the tapping sounds were uneven. It occurred to her that possibly they were a code. She could not translate any of the tapping sounds into words, but on a hunch she stood up, crossed to a bare spot on the floor, and in Morse code tapped out:

"Who are you?"

There was no answer. Nancy waited two minutes before moving. There was not a sound from the basement. Had the tapper left?

Nancy dashed from window to window and looked to see if anyone were hurrying from Miss Carter's. Nobody was in sight.

"That tapper must be in the house still," she concluded.

Although certain that the door from the kitchen to the basement was locked, Nancy went to make doubly sure. The bolt was in place.

She returned to her listening post and sat in the chair for another hour. There was no recurrence of the tapping, so finally Nancy decided to go to bed.

"Tomorrow morning Bess and George and I can investigate the basement thoroughly."

She was just dozing off when a shriek from outdoors awakened her. Nancy rushed to the window of her room, which was in the back of the house. All the lights in the garage were on and she could hear excited voices.

Wondering what had happened, Nancy grabbed her robe and slippers and hurried into the hall. By this time the disturbance had started a couple of dogs in the neighborhood barking.

The din had awakened both Miss Carter and Mrs. Bealing. The nurse rushed into the hall, demanding to know what was going on.

"I don't know," Nancy said as she dashed past the woman and down the back stairs. Mrs. Bealing followed her.

When Nancy opened the outside kitchen door, she saw a man running across the back yard of the house next door. It was too dark to distinguish his features, but he seemed to be rather short and stocky.

Nancy raced after him. By the time she reached the neighbor's driveway onto which he had turned, he was out of sight. The young sleuth went all the way to the street but saw no one. Not a car was parked nor was one leaving the area. Nancy turned back.

"I wonder if he could have been the mysterious tapper at Miss Carter's," she thought. "I wish I'd had a better look at him."

When Nancy reached the garage, Bess and George were telling Mrs. Bealing what had happened.

"I didn't dream it," Bess was saying excitedly. "That side door to the garage was locked but I heard it squeak. When I looked that way, it was being pushed open."

George took up the story. "I was asleep, but when Bess shrieked, I woke up and turned on the light. I saw the door opening. But slowly it closed and the lock snapped shut."

How had the intruder managed to open it? Had he jimmied the lock? Nancy wondered. A quick glance revealed it had not been tampered with. She concluded that the stranger must have used a skeleton key!

"Did you see anyone?" Nancy asked.

Bess and George shook their heads, and George

said, "There was such a commotion among the cats, we didn't have a chance to hunt for whoever tried to get in here."

"I think maybe I saw him," Nancy told her and explained. "Since I lost track of him so soon, he must have scooted around some other houses and disappeared."

The animal uproar continued. Two dogs came bounding into the Carter yard and yelped at the cats in the wire enclosure. The Persians in turn arched their backs and hissed at the tormentors.

"Get out of here!" George shouted at the dogs.

One of them slunk away but the other became defiant. He clawed at the wire cage, and when George rushed outside and tried to yank him away by his collar, he turned and would have sunk his teeth into her arm if she had not pulled it away in time.

Meanwhile, Nancy had found the garden hose. She turned it on and aimed the stream of water at the angry dog. For a few seconds he caught the water in his mouth as if playing with it, then gave up the fight and ran off.

The excited cats refused to settle down. Some had scooted up the sides of the enclosure and were clinging to it. Others had dashed into the garage and hidden under any available object.

Mrs. Bealing was wringing her hands. "I don't think we'll ever get these animals quieted down," she said. "Perhaps I should bring Miss Carter out here."

"That's a good idea," Bess agreed. "I'll help you."

As soon as Miss Carter arrived she began to call each Persian by name.

"Don't be so naughty, Abatha," she said to one.

The ball of fluff clinging to the top of the cage disengaged itself and climbed toward her.

"Come down here, Rosemond," she told another, and it obeyed instantly. The girls were amused by the names and amazed that the woman had such good control over the cats.

"She just loves them," Bess whispered to Nancy. "I should think she'd hate to sell any of her darlings."

At that moment they heard a shout from the house next door. A second-floor window was raised and a man stuck his head out.

"What are you trying to do?" he thundered. "Miss Carter, don't you know people around here want to sleep? I'm not going to put up with those cats of yours any longer! I've stood them for six months."

"I'm dreadfully sorry about what happened," Miss Carter called to him. "It wasn't the cats' fault. Someone tried to break into the garage and that upset them."

"What's that got to do with the dogs?" the man shouted.

"I'm sure it won't happen again, Mr. Bunce," Miss Carter assured him.

"That's a lot of talk!" the man exclaimed. "You're not going to get away with this. I've told you before to get rid of the cats."

Miss Carter looked worried. She said to Nancy, "This is the first disturbance we've had."

The conversation, which was too low for Mr. Bunce to hear, seemed to anger the man. "What are you conniving now?" he cried angrily. "Whatever it is, it won't do you any good!"

Bess stared at the man in disgust. "What a creep he is!" she whispered.

Mr. Bunce continued his tirade. "I'll tell you, Miss Carter, what I'm going to do—inform the authorities these cats are a nuisance and a menace, and I'll see to it that you get rid of them at once!" He slammed the window shut.

Miss Carter had turned ash white. In a tremulous voice she said, "I love my cats and selling them brings me a nice livelihood, which I need. Mr. Bunce will ruin my business!"

Another thought occurred to Nancy. If Miss Carter should decide to move away, the mystery of the stolen cats and the tapper might never be solved. She was determined to clear up both mysteries so this could not happen.

CHAPTER III

Actor's Surprise

ALTHOUGH Bess was a bit fearful she agreed to spend the rest of the night in the garage with George.

"It's very comfortable here," she admitted, "and cooler than inside the house."

Mrs. Bealing made lemonade for the group, then they all went back to bed. At breakfast time Miss Carter insisted upon coming downstairs to the table.

Nancy said to her, "Do you think Mr. Bunce really intends to make trouble?"

Miss Carter shook her head. "He's hot-tempered but I'm sure his bark is worse than his bite. Let's forget him and concentrate on finding the tapper in this house."

"I'm afraid," said Nancy, "that I can't play detective tonight. I must go home for a rehearsal. And there's another one tomorrow night."

"Oh dear!" Mrs. Bealing spoke up. "Bess and George, do you have to go, too?"

"Well, n-o-o-o," Bess said after a pause, "but I hate to stay here without Nancy. I'm not much of a sleuth."

Miss Carter patted the girl's hand. "You were the one who saved my cats last night," she reminded Bess. "If you hadn't awakened, I might have lost several more of my prize Persians."

Flattery had its effect and Bess consented to stay if George would.

"I'm game," her cousin said.

Mrs. Bealing heaved a sigh. "I feel much better now. Thank you."

Miss Carter expressed interest in Nancy's rehearsal. "Is this for a concert or a play?"

"A play. I take the part of a dancer. I don't have many lines, but I do have three tap numbers."

Miss Carter leaned forward across the table. "Nancy, I'm terrifically interested. I used to be an actress myself." She looked off into space. "I loved it and felt sad when I had to retire."

Bess asked what plays Miss Carter had been in.

The actress named several and added, "My greatest role was in *The Dancer and the Fool.* I played the part of the dancer. You know, I believe that with a few changes that play could be modernized and produced right now."

She asked Nancy, "Have you ever thought seriously of going on the stage? You'd be perfect in the role I played."

Nancy laughed. Before she had a chance to answer, Bess said, "Nancy wouldn't give up her detective work for anything. Now and then she does other things, like this play, but she spends most of her time solving mysteries."

Miss Carter smiled. As she was about to make a comment, the telephone rang. Mrs. Bealing answered and said that the police wanted to speak to her patient. The actress was wheeled to the hall and picked up the phone.

She listened for a few minutes, then said, "Oh, the poor thing! That was wicked! . . . Yes, I'll send somebody to pick up the kitten. And how are we going to find the person who did this?" She went on to tell about the attempted intrusion the night before.

There was another long pause, then she said, "All right. I'll sleep better if I know the police will stop here regularly on their rounds."

When Miss Carter came back to the table she reported that laboratory tests had shown that the "sleepy" kitten had indeed been drugged. There was no doubt now in anyone's mind that the thief who had taken the five older cats had also drugged them.

"I'll be glad to run over and get the kitten," Bess said.

"I'd certainly appreciate it if you would," Miss Carter said.

During Bess's absence, Nancy and George went to the basement hoping to find a clue that would explain the reason for the tapping sounds. Nancy carried a flashlight in her left hand, a small hammer in her right. The girls found the two small windows and outside door bolted shut.

"First, let's look directly under that chair where I was sitting last night," she suggested.

George was carrying a small stepladder. She set it in place and Nancy climbed up. Seeing nothing suspicious, she tapped lightly with the hammer to detect any hollow spots.

"It all sounds the same to me," George commented. "Do you think the mysterious tapper was hunting for some secret hiding place in the ceiling of the basement?"

Nancy shrugged. "I haven't the faintest idea," she replied. "I have been wondering, though, whether or not he and the fellow who broke into the garage are the same man."

She explained that this possibility had occurred to her because there had been such a short interval between the two mysterious events.

"Frankly," Nancy went on, "I'm amazed that he would dare make so much noise with people in the house."

"Maybe," George speculated, "he wants to be thought of as a ghost and scare everyone away."

"He won't succeed," Nancy declared. "Well, let's get on with our investigation."

The two girls made a minute search of the ceiling, side walls, and floor. They found no indication of an opening in the paneled walls or in the cement floor.

"Perhaps," said George, "the tapper is a nut and just comes here to have fun scaring people."

"I'm sure there's more to it than that," Nancy replied.

By the time she and George went upstairs, Bess had returned with the kitten. They all patted the little animal, which had recovered completely and was very frisky.

Miss Carter had been taken to her bedroom, so the pet was carried up there. She fondled the kitten lovingly, then asked Mrs. Bealing to put it out in the garage.

The nurse went off. As she descended the stairway, the front doorbell rang. The others heard her open the door but almost instantly close it again. Then she carried the kitten out the back door before returning to the second floor.

"Who rang the bell?" Miss Carter asked her.

Mrs. Bealing smiled. "A tall, handsome gray-haired man. Too bad he had the wrong house. He wanted to know if a Miss Violette lived here."

"What!" Miss Carter exclaimed. "Oh, find him! Find him! He wants me! I'm Miss Violette!"

The others stared at the actress and finally Mrs. Bealing said, "I'm sorry. You never told me your name was Miss Violette."

Tears came to Miss Carter's eyes. She opened a bureau drawer and pulled out a picture.

"He's the one," Mrs. Bealing said. "Only he's older looking now."

Miss Carter cried out, "He was the man who played the part of the fool in the play I told you about. He and I were going to be married and through an odd circumstance we became separated and now I've lost him again!"

Instantly Nancy sprang into action. "We'll try to find him for you, Miss Carter. Did he have a car, Mrs. Bealing?"

"Yes, a bright-red convertible."

As the three girls dashed down the steps, Bess said, "Oh, isn't this romantic and exciting!"

Suddenly it occurred to Nancy that they did not know the man's name and she hurried back upstairs to find out. "He's Toby Simpson," Miss Carter told her.

"Which way did he go, Mrs. Bealing?" Nancy asked quickly.

"Toward Main Street."

By the time Nancy reached the car, Bess had it running. She slid over and Nancy got behind the wheel. The convertible sped down Amity Place. When it reached the intersection of Main

Street, Nancy stopped and the girls looked in both directions.

"I see a bright-red convertible!" George said, pointing to the right.

Nancy drove as fast as she dared. The car she was chasing had the top down. The man at the wheel was threading his way expertly through the traffic.

"Oh, we mustn't lose him!" Bess urged.

Nancy was doing her best to catch up with the gray-haired Toby Simpson, but as she came to a signal light, it turned red. The convertible had gone ahead and was making good speed.

The girls chafed under the delay and the instant the light became green Nancy shot ahead. By now the chase was hopeless. Toby Simpson and his car had disappeared, and though the girls rode up and down various streets, they could not find the red convertible.

Bess sighed. "What luck! Mr. Simpson has probably gone out of town, never to return. Poor Miss Carter!"

When the girls gave Miss Carter the disappointing news, the actress sighed deeply. Apparently she did not want to discuss the unfortunate happening and changed the subject.

"Did you detectives find anything in the basement?" she asked.

"No," Nancy replied, "but this afternoon I

want to look around the second floor and up in your attic."

Mrs. Bealing revealed that she had heard muffled tapping sounds from the third floor.

"Then let's go up there first," George proposed.

Miss Carter said with a smile, "Don't be too surprised at what you find."

The three girls were not prepared for the amazing assortment of objects stored in the attic. Evidently Miss Carter had collected souvenirs from various plays in which she had appeared. There were chests, a battered white wooden horse, forms with costumes on them and covered with plastic bags, and a mummy case standing upright.

"O-oh, this place gives me the creeps," Bess remarked. "I could almost imagine some of the figures coming to life."

Nancy suggested that the girls separate and each hunt for a clue to the tapper or to what he might be looking for.

It was not long before Nancy found a crossbeam in a side wall which, she thought, was not necessary to the construction of the building. She tugged at it and presently the beam came away. One part of the underside had been hollowed out into a square and the lack of dust in the empty space indicated that something had recently been removed from it.

"A square box, I'm sure," Nancy told herself.

She called Bess and George over and pointed out her discovery.

George remarked, "When Mrs. Bealing heard the tapper, he must have been hammering lightly on the beam to pull it loose. I wonder what was hidden in it."

"We must find out who lived in this house be-before Miss Carter," Nancy said. She glanced at her watch. "It's getting late. I'll have to leave in a few moments. Do you girls want to continue looking or come downstairs with me?"

Bess and George said they had had enough sleuthing for one day. Besides, they had promised to help feed the cats and give them fresh water.

When Nancy told Miss Carter about the movable beam, the actress was amazed. She had purchased the house from people named Smith who had not lived there long. A lawyer had attended to everything, and Miss Carter did not know who the previous owners were.

"But I'll try to find out," she said.

Nancy said good-by to everyone and went to her car, which was parked in the driveway. As she pulled into the street and turned in the direction of River Heights, she noticed a black sedan behind her. It followed her down the street. When Nancy reached the highway out of town, the same car was still behind her.

At first Nancy thought this was merely a coincidence, but as she rode along, it occurred to her that the man, whom she could not see very well, was deliberately following her. She went down a street in a new housing development, then turned, and came back to the main road. The other driver did the same.

"I'm sure now that he's after me," Nancy thought. "I'd better not take any shortcuts or deserted roads." She jammed on her brakes, so the trailing car came closer rather suddenly and she caught a glimpse of a pudgy, double-chinned man. He looked to be in his mid-twenties.

"I certainly don't know him," Nancy thought. "Could he be the tapper or the cat thief?"

She made a mental note of the license number of his car. "I'll find out who he is!" she determined.

As they neared River Heights, the young detective decided that somehow she must shake her pursuer. She watched for an opportunity.

CHAPTER IV

Car Thief

INSTINCT told Nancy not to go directly home.

"No doubt that man behind me wants to find out where I live," she said to herself. "Well, I won't let him!"

She knew that anyone could find out from the license bureau who owned the car, but this would not necessarily prove that the driver was also the owner. Turning abruptly down a side street, she headed for a parking lot.

Nancy quickly found a spot, locked the convertible, and started making her way among the many parked cars. Glancing over her shoulder, she saw her pursuer looking vainly for her out of his window. She smiled that her ruse had worked, then headed for her father's office.

"I'll tell Dad what happened and get his advice about this."

To avoid detection Nancy rode in the elevator

to a floor above, and walked down one flight to Mr. Drew's office.

"If that pudgy man saw me come into the building, I guess he's pretty confused by this time."

Mr. Drew's secretary, Miss Hanson, looked surprised but glad to see Nancy. "Hi!" she greeted her. "Something's on your mind—I can see it in your eyes."

Nancy laughed. "You're right. I've just shaken off a man who was following me."

Miss Hanson gasped. "How terrible! You did the right thing coming here. Your father has a client in his office but I think the man will be leaving any minute. Please sit down and tell me about your new mystery."

Nancy had just started to explain when the door of her father's office opened. Mr. Drew shook hands with his client, saying he would call him in a couple of days. Then he turned to Nancy.

"Hello, dear. Nice to see you, but I have a feeling this isn't a social call." His eyes twinkled.

When Nancy reported what had happened to her since leaving Miss Carter's home, the lawyer frowned.

"I don't like this," he said. "As you said, the man can trace you. But we'll even things up. I'll call the license bureau right away to find out who this pudgy individual is and if he has tried to trace your license."

Mr. Drew asked Miss Hanson to put in the call

and soon he was talking to a man at the motor vehicle bureau. Within a short time he had his answer.

"The name of the owner is Barton Trask," he told Nancy. "Barton is a friend of mine. . . . Miss Hanson, will you please phone him."

While Miss Hanson dialed the number, Mr. Drew said to Nancy, "So far, my dear, no one has tried to get information on you at the bureau. I've instructed the men there to withhold your address in that event."

The ensuing conversation between the lawyer and his friend proved to be enlightening. Mr. Trask said that his car had been stolen several weeks ago and had been sold by the thief, using a forged certificate of ownership. Apparently the thief had transferred the stolen license plate to another car.

"I'll notify the police and the license bureau about all of this," Mr. Drew said. He looked steadily at Nancy. "You've proven to me many times you know how to take care of yourself, but I can't help worrying about you. Right now I think it would be best if Miss Hanson drives you home. Later I'll bring your car and make sure no one is following me."

Nancy opened her purse and handed over the key. She smiled at her father. "Thanks a million, Dad. And don't forget, early dinner tonight. I have a rehearsal for the play."

"I'll be there."

Soon after Nancy arrived home she received a phone call from Chief McGinnis of the River Heights Police Department. He told her that his men were still looking for the thief who had taken Mr. Trask's car. He asked for a full description of the man who had followed Nancy.

"I'm afraid it can't be very full," she replied, "because I saw him only behind the wheel of his car. He appeared to be pudgy, double-chinned, and had a small nose. His hair was dark and he had a good deal of it. He was so far down in the seat I'd say he's short."

"That helps," the chief said. Then he chuckled. "I suppose he's part of the new mystery on which you're working."

"I'm not sure," Nancy replied, "but I suspect he may be."

A few minutes later, as she was about to take a shower, the telephone rang again. This time a man's high-pitched voice said, "Miss Nancy Drew?"

"Yes. Who are you?" Nancy asked.

"I'll tell you when I come," the stranger replied. "I think you know some secrets I have to have. You stay there in your house. I'll be right over to get them from you." The man hung up.

As Nancy stood lost in thought, Hannah Gruen came to her side. "Who was that?" she asked.

"I don't know, Hannah. Some man with a high

squeaky voice. He sounds ominous. I wonder if he's the man who followed me from Berryville."

"Oh dear!" The housekeeper sighed. "Nancy, you just seem to go from one dangerous adventure to another. What did this man want?"

Nancy managed a wan smile. "He said I have some secrets he has to have and he'll be right over to get them."

Hannah Gruen bristled. "He will, will he? Well, we'll not let him in! And that's final!"

Nancy hugged the housekeeper. "I won't argue with you, but I would like to know who he is."

"Never mind about that," Hannah said firmly. "We'll pull down all the shades so he can't look in."

Nancy puckered her lips. "And you won't even let me take a peek to see who he is?"

"Not even a peek. Let him think he has the wrong house or anything else he wants to figure out."

"I'll leave everything to you," Nancy said with a little smile. "Now I'm going for a nice warm shower and get ready for the rehearsal."

She had just started dressing when the front doorbell rang. No one answered. It rang again.

Nancy waited to see what Hannah would do. She remained resolute in her resolve. The caller pushed the button for the third time and kept his finger on the bell. It rang for a whole minute, then finally the person gave up.

"Just the same I wish I knew who that was," Nancy thought.

She finished dressing and came downstairs to help Hannah with the dinner. As Nancy passed through the front hall, the telephone rang. Was the man with the high squeaky voice calling again?

"I'd better answer, anyway," Nancy decided. "It might be Dad and he'll be worried if he gets no answer."

Nancy picked up the phone and said hello in a low voice.

"Nancy?" Then the caller went on, "Remember me? I'm supposed to have a date with you tonight to take you to the rehearsal."

"Ned!" Nancy shouted. The relief in her voice as well as her delight were very evident to Ned Nickerson, an Emerson College student and star football player, whom she dated frequently.

"What's going on?" he asked. "I arrived early and rang and rang your bell but nobody would let me in. I'm at your neighbor's, Mrs. Humphrey. She was sure something awful must have happened to you."

Nancy laughed. "I'm perfectly all right and so is Hannah. Come on over and I'll tell you why the shades are down and we wouldn't let anybody in."

"Okay. I'll do a little staccato on your doorbell so you'll know who it is."

Within five minutes the handsome, dark-haired Ned walked in. "Can't wait to hear the reason for all this secrecy," he said after greeting Nancy warmly.

When Ned heard about the demand made by the mysterious caller he became alarmed. "Nancy, if this ties in with a new mystery of yours, don't you think you should give it up?"

When Nancy did not answer, Ned shrugged. "I suppose there's no use asking you that. Well, where does the mystery stand now?"

While she was telling him about the ghostly tapper and the cat thief, she kept wondering if the strange caller would arrive. But another half-hour went by and he did not appear.

Finally Nancy chuckled. "Ned, I believe you kept that other man away from here. Thanks a lot."

The couple heard Mr. Drew's key in the front door and soon afterward everyone was seated at the dinner table. Hannah had prepared a delicious meal of roast lamb, peas, and raspberry tarts.

Conversation was almost entirely about the mystery. When Nancy and Ned were ready to leave the house to attend the rehearsal, Mr. Drew suggested that the two exchange cars after they returned home. He added, "It might keep that man in the black sedan off your trail, Nancy."

"Glad to do it, Mr. Drew," Ned said, and Nancy nodded in agreement.

"Another thing, Nancy," her father said. "Whenever you leave this house, I want you to wear dark glasses and a scarf that completely covers your head. It may be an unnecessary precaution, but please do it for me." Nancy kissed her father and went upstairs to get a scarf and sunglasses.

When she and Ned reached the high school auditorium where the rehearsal was to be held, Ned seated himself about halfway down the center aisle. Nancy went up the steps that led to the stage.

Several members of the cast were rushing around, some mumbling their lines to themselves, others reading from the script. The orchestra was tuning up and the director was giving last-minute instructions to the actors and actresses.

The play was a variety show with a thin thread of plot running through it. Nancy was to appear three times in tap numbers; once in the first act in a dialogue with a young man. In the second she would dance with a group of girls. First each one would perform an intricate step, then dance together.

Just before the finale, in which everyone would sing, Nancy was to perform her solo.

The director, Mr. Skank, was very exacting. By the time the first act had been rehearsed over and over, nearly two hours had gone by.

"We'll be here all night," complained a girl standing near Nancy.

"It looks so. But I hope not. A friend of mine is waiting for me. Poor boy! He has a long drive after he takes me home. Maybe the second act will go faster."

It was not long before the group of dancers came onstage and one by one the girls began to perform their numbers. Soon it would be Nancy's turn.

She glanced out into the auditorium just in time to see Ned leave his seat hurriedly. Her eyes followed him up the aisle and into the corridor. As Ned emerged into the hallway, a pudgy man jumped him and shot a well-aimed blow at Ned's jaw!

CHAPTER V

Mysterious Key

"Miss Drew, what's the matter?" Mr. Skank cried out. "It's your turn. Dance!"

Nancy paid no attention. She dashed across the stage, leaped down the steps, and ran up the center aisle of the auditorium to the main corridor.

As she burst through the door and looked down the hallway, she recognized Ned's assailant as the pudgy man who had followed her in the black sedan.

He was reeling from a blow Ned had delivered, but the man retaliated with a swift punch that staggered Ned. Seeing Nancy, the intruder ran out the front door.

She hurried after him, but by the time Nancy had covered the distance to the outside of the building, he was not in sight. She knew it was hopeless to try finding him and disappointedly returned to the corridor.

"Ned, what happened?" she asked. "And are you all right?"

He smiled grimly. "Yes. That fellow sure delivers a mean uppercut," he said.

Nancy asked Ned why he had left the auditorium so hurriedly. He said that a boy had come down the aisle and handed him a hand-printed note. Ned pulled it from his pocket and gave it to Nancy to read.

You are to get out of the picture. Nancy Drew has another steady now. Come to the corridor and you will find out.

"Of course I went to see what it was all about," Ned explained. "That pudgy guy let go with a punch and knocked me off balance. But what brought you to the corridor?"

"I just happened to see that punch," she replied. "I feel responsible, Ned, and I'm dreadfully sorry."

Ned grinned. "Just so long as you don't have another steady date, I'll forgive you for anything."

Nancy laughed. "Thanks. Ned, why don't you go to my house and put something on that jaw? Dad can pick me up later."

"Nothing doing. I'll go find some ice water in this building and doctor myself. You go back to rehearsal. That director must be furious."

As Nancy turned to leave she noticed a key on the floor.

"Is this yours, Ned?" she asked.

"No. When I knocked that man down, the key must have fallen out of his pocket."

"It looks like a car key," Nancy said. "The key might lead to your attacker. Ned, will you call the police and ask them to come here?"

"All right."

There was a telephone booth nearby and he headed for it while Nancy went back to the auditorium. When she returned to the stage, Mr. Skank had some pretty harsh words for her.

He ended by saying, "I don't relish staying here all night and you've certainly held up the works, Miss Drew."

Before Nancy had a chance to explain, one of the girls in the cast called out, "You don't know it, Mr. Skank, but Nancy is an amateur detective. She probably had to leave in a hurry in connection with some case."

"Is that true?" the director asked.

Nancy nodded but did not offer any other explanation. Mr. Skank made no further comment about the interruption. "Do your dance, Miss Drew. Music, please."

Nancy, desiring to make amends for her sudden leave-taking, performed perfectly. Grudgingly Mr. Skank praised her.

The rest of the rehearsal went smoothly. Nancy felt that in her final tap number she had not danced so well as she could. She mentioned this to Ned as they started for home.

"I didn't notice anything wrong," he said, "but if you weren't satisfied, I'm sure it was a combination of weariness and excitement. You've had a big day!"

Nancy had to admit that it did seem long and she was ready for a good night's sleep. When they arrived at the Drew home, Nancy's father was watching a late movie on TV.

He looked at Ned and asked, "Were you in an accident?"

"No, Mr. Drew, but I had a chance to wallop that guy who was following Nancy this afternoon."

The lawyer grinned. "Good for you. Did you put him in the hospital?"

"Wish I had," Ned responded, then explained what had happened.

Mr. Drew insisted that Ned stay overnight. The young man accepted and said he must be off very early in the morning.

"But I'll be back tomorrow night to take Nancy to the rehearsal," he added.

Hannah Gruen quickly prepared a snack and then announced that she knew just the thing to put on Ned's jaw. She went to get a soothing lotion and soaked a bandage with it.

"Keep this wet compress on all night and I

guarantee that tomorrow morning you'll look like yourself again," she said.

The housekeeper's prediction came true. Breakfast was served early and Ned showed no effects of his fight with the pudgy man except one little black-and-blue mark on his cheek. Hannah was pleased and said she had used a homemade remedy of hers that never failed.

Ned smiled. "Maybe you should patent it and go into business. Quick cure! Quick money!"

"I'll think about it," Mrs. Gruen said, chuckling.

Ned left in a few minutes and Nancy helped Hannah with some household chores. Then she set off for Berryville in Ned's car. On the way she stopped at River Heights Police Headquarters to find out if the officers had traced the owner of the key she had picked up at the high school. Sergeant Rothman, who was on duty, said that it had been determined it was not a car key and he doubted that anyone would claim it.

"Would you like it back?" he asked Nancy.

"Yes, I would." She had a strong hunch that the key might lead to something important in regard to the pudgy man.

Nancy put the key in her purse and left headquarters. When she arrived at Miss Carter's, Nancy parked Ned's car in front of the garage.

Hearing voices inside the building, she called out, "Hi! I'm back!"

Bess and George greeted her as she stepped into the garage.

"How's everything?" Nancy asked.

Bess heaved a sigh. "Okay, but I'm so tired of opening cans of cat food, I never want to see another one in my whole life."

"Let me help you," Nancy said. "Suppose you girls take a rest while I serve the cats their breakfast and you tell me about your evening."

George grinned. "All we can report is a big zero. No thieves, no tappers, no prowlers, no intruders, not even a mouse. How about the rehearsal, Nancy?"

When Nancy finished telling about her eventful evening, the cousins looked at each other in amazement. George remarked, "Wouldn't you know Nancy would have all the excitement?"

"That suits me," said Bess. "I got a good night's sleep and have nothing to worry about."

Nancy went into the house to put on blue jeans, loafers, and a shirt so she could help Bess and George clean the cage. It took them until late morning and Bess declared she was absolutely starved.

"I hope Mrs. Bealing has a good lunch for us," she said, leading the way into the kitchen. "Umm! Chicken salad with fresh tomatoes. And girls, look at that big, big chocolate cake!"

"Bess Marvin," George said severely, "you leave that chocolate cake alone. Every time you take off a few pounds, you put them right back on."

Bess looked at the cake wistfully. Should she pay attention to George who, she knew, was right, or should she enjoy the luscious dessert?

To herself she said, "I won't decide now. Maybe—just maybe—I'll be satisfied with the chicken salad and a little bitsy piece of cake."

This did not prove to be the case and later when Bess cut a slice for herself it was so wide that even Miss Carter had to laugh. She eased the tension, however, by saying, "I've always felt that the place to diet is in one's own home, not in someone else's."

Bess beamed at her. "I could hug you for that, Miss Carter."

After lunch the actress was carried upstairs for her nap. The girls helped Mrs. Bealing with the luncheon dishes, then the nurse said she would like to run downtown.

"A kind neighbor across the street has offered to take me shopping. Will you girls please answer the phone and the doorbell."

"Yes, indeed," Nancy replied, and Bess added, "Bring home something extra special to eat, will you?" Mrs. Bealing laughed.

When she had gone, Nancy suggested that the girls go to the basement once more to try to find out why the tapper had been there.

"I'm sure he was hunting for something," she

said, and reminded the others about the mysterious telephone caller. "He may have meant secrets to do with this house."

She led the way to the basement. The door to the kitchen was left open so they could hear anyone who might call.

A second intensive search of the room was begun. Except for occasional conversation among the girls there was total silence in the house.

They were investigating a far corner when Bess suddenly grabbed Nancy's arm. "I hear it!" she said in a hushed voice. "The tapping! It's upstairs somewhere!"

On tiptoe the girls dashed to the steps and rushed up to the kitchen.

CHAPTER VI

The Secret Room

THE three girls quickly went through all the first-floor rooms, opening closet doors along the way. No one was hiding and there were no visible footprints or fingerprints to indicate that anyone from the outside had sneaked in.

"The tapping must have come from the second floor," Nancy whispered. "I wonder if Miss Carter heard it or if she's asleep."

Bess and George went up the back stairway to the second floor, while Nancy took the front. Each bedroom was investigated but there was not a sign of an intruder. Finally they arrived at Miss Carter's closed door. No sound came from within.

"Even if she's asleep, I think we should wake her up," Nancy said.

She knocked and in a few seconds the actress's sleepy voice called, "Come in."

She was still in bed. At once Nancy apologized

for having awakened her. "We heard tapping sounds in the house. Were you knocking on the wall?"

"No, my dear."

"Did you hear the tapping sounds?" George asked the actress.

Miss Carter gave the girl a most engaging smile. "When I take a nap, I'm practically unconscious," she replied.

Bess said feelingly, "Please go back to sleep. When you wake up, I'll bring you tea and cookies."

"That's very sweet of you," Miss Carter said.

The girls retreated and closed the door. In the hall Nancy reminded her friends that the tapper might have been up on the third floor but had come down and escaped from the house before they had left Miss Carter's room. They went up to the attic and walked around.

"Nothing here," said George.

"Maybe not," Nancy replied, "but somebody has been in this attic."

"How do you know?" Bess spoke up.

"That chest has been moved," Nancy answered. "I'm positive it was over here before."

The girls shifted several other objects, hoping to find a clue to the mystery. But they saw no trace of a trap door or loose boards.

"Well, I guess it's back to the basement," George said. "Okay, Nancy?"

"Okay."

When they reached the basement, Nancy stood in the center of the floor and slowly turned in circles. Bess and George watched their friend in fascination. They knew enough not to ask what was going through her mind.

Presently Nancy stopped turning and walked over to the rear wall of the basement. She tapped on the panels.

"Girls," she said, "do you realize that this basement is not so large as the first floor of the house?"

"I hadn't noticed," Bess replied. "But what you say isn't unusual, is it? Lots of people have a small cellar compared to the size of their house."

Suddenly Nancy said, "Wait here."

She dashed up the stairs and outdoors. The young sleuth walked round and round the house examining the foundation. Finally she went back to the basement, and beamed her flashlight inch by inch along the rear wall.

"What do you suspect?" George finally asked, curiosity getting the better of her.

"An opening in this wall," Nancy answered. "Suppose you girls start at the other end and hunt for a clue."

Just before they all reached the center of the wall, Bess exclaimed, "Here's a place that looks as if a rat had gnawed it!"

Nancy studied the edge of the beveled board.

She tried pulling it forward with her fingernails. Though it moved a fraction of an inch, she could not budge it any farther.

George was already looking around for a tool and found one made of steel with a hooked end. It was lying on a shelf above the panel. She inserted the hook in the gouged-out spot.

"Be careful!" Bess warned. "We don't know what may be behind that wood. Some hidden object could shoot out and harm us!"

George had dug the hook deep into the wood and with Nancy's help the panel began to move. When it turned at right angles to the wall, Nancy shone her flashlight beyond. The three girls gasped. Before them was a fully furnished bedroom.

"The bed has been slept in recently!" Bess exclaimed.

"It's a secret room!" Nancy cried out. "Oh, girls, this is a wonderful clue!"

There was a switch just inside the movable panel which illuminated three lamps. An open door to one side revealed a fully furnished bathroom. Nancy hurried inside and felt a towel and washcloth.

"They're damp!" she called. "Someone has been here very recently. I'm sure this is the hideout of the tapper."

"And here's his razor," said George, rushing in.

Bess admitted that she was frightened. "The

intruder certainly has a key to this house," she declared. "I think all the locks should be changed at once."

Nancy agreed. Bess offered to go tell Miss Carter even if she had to awaken her again.

"And I'll attend to getting a locksmith to come here this very afternoon," she added.

After Bess had left, Nancy and George searched the small bedroom for clues to the identity of the occupant. There was a cot and along one wall stood a highboy. On another was a series of cupboards that reached from the floor to the ceiling. One had a grill metal front but the others were of solid wood. All the doors were locked. The girls opened the highboy drawers but found nothing inside.

George stared at the cupboards. "I sure wish we could get a look inside."

"I wonder," said Nancy, "if by any chance that pudgy man lives in this room and the key he dropped might open these cupboards. I'll get it."

She went upstairs and took the key from her purse. Nancy was back in a few minutes and inserted the key in the lock.

"It fits!" she exclaimed.

One by one the cupboards were opened. There were several books in one; the others held boxes of letters and other papers.

"These are all addressed to William Woonton

"It's a secret room!" Nancy cried out

at this address," Nancy said, after examining several.

"And here's a diary," George spoke up, lifting a book from underneath a pile of papers. "It says *Diary of Gus Woonton.*"

The girls began to turn the leaves of the diary. The notations were startling. They told of Gus Woonton being kept prisoner in the windowless room with only a small duct in the ceiling for fresh air.

One item read: "This is the work of my crazy guardians who are taking care of me while my parents are traveling for a year. My guardians declare I'm crazy and have to be locked up, but it is the other way around. But I'll get square with them. Every time they let me out of here, I'll take—"

The sentence was not finished, and though the girls scanned the book thoroughly, they could find no clue as to how Gus was getting square with his guardians or what he planned to take.

"Do you suppose," said George, "that the pudgy man could be Gus Woonton? And he's the tapper?"

"Anything is possible," Nancy replied. "I wonder where he goes when he isn't in this room."

Without waiting for a response from George, she went on, "I guess we'd better lock this cupboard and close that panel into the other part of the basement." She chuckled. "Poor Gus! When he comes here for another night's sleep, he won't be able to get in."

"Why not?" George asked. "He can use this same hook he always does."

Nancy smiled. "We'll take the key and the tool upstairs and hide them. I suppose this room is where the tapper hides. Now maybe we or the police will be able to nab him."

George and Nancy went to Miss Carter's room. Mrs. Bealing had returned. Both women were astounded at the discovery the girl detectives had made. But Miss Carter could throw no light on Gus Woonton or his parents or guardians.

"I'll call my lawyer, Carl Amberson, at once and ask him who owned the house before the Smiths did," she said.

The girls were near the phone and could hear Mr. Amberson's voice very clearly. Not only was he surprised at the strange happenings, but said that the William Woontons had indeed owned the house at one time.

"I did not know they had a son Gus and I have no idea where they might be. I'll try to find out, though, and let you know."

After Miss Carter finished speaking with Mr. Amberson, Nancy asked permission to turn this part of the mystery over to her father.

"He has traced many lost persons," she said.

The actress agreed and Nancy telephoned Mr.

Drew. He, too, was amazed at the turn of events and promised to do what he could.

A few minutes later Bess arrived with a locksmith. The man worked for over an hour to change all the locks, including those on the garage, then went off.

"Now I feel safer," Bess said with a sigh as she turned over the keys to Miss Carter.

They were about to start preparations for dinner when the telephone rang. Mr. Drew was calling Nancy.

"I have some very important information for you," he said. "I think you'd better come home as soon as possible. And be sure to bring the diary and the cupboard key with you."

CHAPTER VII

The Runaway

"CAN'T you tell me now what you found out?" Nancy asked her father.

He laughed. "I think the matter should be kept secret for the present. Anyway, I'd rather not discuss it on the telephone. Here's more news. The Faynes and Marvins want Bess and George to come home. There's a special family party being held out of town tonight that they're to attend."

Nancy was a bit alarmed about leaving Miss Carter and Mrs. Bealing alone. Apparently Mr. Drew guessed her thought.

"I know you don't want to desert the Amity Place mystery," he said, "so I have persuaded Hannah to stay with Miss Carter while you girls have to be away. She'll take a taxi out there."

"Oh, Dad, you think of everything!" Nancy said.

Mr. Drew told her a client was waiting so he

would have to say good-by. "I'll see you later."

Nancy gave his message to Bess and George. Mrs. Bealing was delighted to hear that her friend Hannah Gruen was coming to spend a little time at Miss Carter's. "She's such a capable person to have around."

"She certainly is," Nancy agreed.

Bess and George had exchanged guilty glances. Both admitted they had completely forgotten the family party!

George said, "Nancy, you always pick up such fascinating mysteries, you make us forget our duties to aunts and uncles and cousins!"

Nancy chuckled. "Sorry, girls. Maybe you can pick up a clue at the party. Ask your relatives if they ever knew or heard of people named Woonton who used to live in Berryville."

"Will do," George promised.

The three girls went back to the basement and opened the panel to the secret room. Nancy unlocked the wall cabinet and took out the diary. Then she relocked the cupboard, and the panel was closed again.

Since Bess and George did not know when they would be able to return, they decided to pack all their clothes and take them home. "I'd enjoy a change of slacks and blouses, anyway," said Bess.

The cousins had just finished packing when Bess called out, "I heard a car door slam. Perhaps it's Mrs. Gruen arriving."

The bell rang and Nancy hurried to the front door. Hannah Gruen stood there, a broad smile on her face.

"Nancy," she said, "this is the first time I've ever tried to substitute for you in solving a mystery."

As Nancy gave the housekeeper a hug, she said, "Who knows? Maybe you'll solve it while I'm gone."

"Not much likelihood of that," Hannah replied, shaking her head.

Nancy took Mrs. Gruen's bag and led the way up the stairs to the second floor. Mrs. Bealing greeted her old friend affectionately. Then Hannah was taken to meet Miss Carter.

"I'm sorry you've been having so much trouble," the Drews' housekeeper said to her.

The actress smiled. "It's said that bad luck comes in threes. I've had mine—first a broken leg, then a mysterious tapper, and finally stolen cats."

Mrs. Gruen remarked that with all the locks on the house changed, she did not see how anyone could get inside.

"And I believe the person who came to steal your Persians the second time got a good scare. I doubt that he'll be back."

Hannah's assurances made Miss Carter feel better at once. Soon the three women were engaged in a lively conversation. Nancy, Bess, and George left quietly.

"When are you going to get your own car back?" George asked Nancy as they rode off in Ned's convertible.

"I don't know. Ned's coming to take me to the rehearsal."

When the girls reached Bess's home, Nancy asked the cousins to call her when they were ready to return to Miss Carter's. She dropped George at the Fayne house, and a few minutes later pulled into her own driveway.

As she unlocked the kitchen door, the place seemed very different. For an instant Nancy wondered why, then realized she missed the fragrant scent of cooking food. There was always a lingering aroma of some special concoction of Hannah's in the air.

"It's just not the same without her here," Nancy thought wistfully.

Within a few minutes Mr. Drew drove in. While Nancy was preparing dinner from a menu Hannah had left, the lawyer related what he had found out about the Woontons.

"Through a stroke of luck I got the information from a lawyer friend of mine who is the attorney for the Beverly, a private hospital. It takes boys and young men who are having mental problems of one sort or another.

"One of their patients was named Gus Woonton. At the time his parents put him there, they were living in Berryville. I haven't found out anything yet as to where Mr. and Mrs. William Woonton went after they sold their house."

Nancy was excited. "Is this Gus Woonton well enough to be interviewed?" she asked.

Mr. Drew's answer was a surprise. "Gus Woonton ran away from the Beverly several weeks ago and there hasn't been any trace of him since that time."

"Oh!" Nancy exclaimed.

She told her father of her suspicion that the man using the secret bedroom and bath in the basement of Miss Carter's house might be Gus Woonton.

"And he might be the tapper," she added.

"You could be right, Nancy. That pudgy man who followed you and who attacked Ned at the school fits the description of the Gus Woonton who ran away. He had a penchant for running away since the time he was a little boy."

"You mean running away from home?" Nancy asked.

Her father nodded. "Yes, and also from school and camp, and at times from hotels when the family was on a trip. When Gus reached his late teens, he became worse, so his parents finally took him to the Beverly."

"What about the guardians?" Nancy asked.

"There was no mention of them. But the Beverly's lawyer promised to call me if he finds out anything more about the William Woontons."

"And there are no clues as to where Gus was running to this time?" Nancy queried.

"Not one, and I think your guess is as good as anybody else's," her father remarked. "Tonight we'll have the police keep an even closer watch on Miss Carter's house. Since all the locks on the entrance doors have been changed, the tapper won't be able to get inside. The officers can close in quickly and grab him if he comes to the house."

As Nancy continued preparing the meal, she and her father speculated about whether or not Gus Woonton lived in the house regularly or just slept there once in a while. And was he the tapper? If so, why was he tapping? Was he just acting spooky to annoy the people in the house, hoping to get them out? Or was there a more sinister motive behind his actions?

Just as dinner was ready, the bell rang. Ned Nickerson had arrived. At once he asked Nancy if she had solved the mystery.

"It's not solved, but we have some good clues," she replied, and briefed him on the latest developments.

"Sounds like progress all right," he commented.

After the meal was over and the kitchen had been tidied, Nancy and Ned had to hurry to make the rehearsal on time.

As they walked into the school a few minutes later, he said, "Tonight, instead of sitting in the auditorium, I think I'll play detective and walk around the corridors to keep a lookout for that pudgy fellow."

They separated and Nancy went up to the stage. Ned made sure that the front door was securely locked as well as all the side entrances. On one of his trips into the corridor back of the stage, he thought he smelled smoke.

"It seems to be coming from under the stage," Ned decided, and opened the door to a stairway. He ran down the steps.

A thin wisp of smoke was coming from the prop room next to the dressing rooms. A fire extinguisher hung on the wall. He grabbed it. Turning the heavy spray can over, he sent a volume of foam onto a pile of clothes which were on fire in the center of the floor.

"I hope this does it," he thought.

In the meantime Nancy found herself with a fifteen-minute recess from the rehearsal.

"I'll see if Ned has learned anything," she told herself, and went out into the corridor back of the stage.

As she neared the doorway to the basement, Nancy smelled smoke. She hurried down the stairway and saw Ned busy with the extinguisher.

"Oh, Nancy, I'm glad you've come. I'm afraid this is too much of a blaze for me to put out alone."

Nancy agreed. "I'd better call the fire department right away."

"Good idea," Ned replied.

She dashed up the stairway and turned the knob on the door which had closed. It was locked!

Frantically Nancy knocked on the door but she had little hope that anyone would hear her. The orchestra was playing loudly.

Nevertheless, she thumped until her knuckles hurt. Still no one came to open the door!

CHAPTER VIII

Missing Diary

FOR a moment Nancy panicked. The situation was desperate. She and Ned must get out of the basement!

She continued to pound her fists on the door and yell as loudly as she could. But the orchestra was still playing a lively number and it drowned out her frantic cries.

"Maybe there's another exit from the prop room," Nancy told herself.

Though the smoke was now thick, she went back down the stairs. Her smarting eyes caught sight of another fire extinguisher hanging on the wall. She grabbed it off the hook.

Before using it, Nancy ran into the powder room and held two towels under a faucet. When they were soaking wet, she hurried to Ned's side and handed one to him. He quickly tied it over his nose and mouth, while Nancy put the other one across hers.

"Are the firemen coming? Let's get out of here!" Ned said grimly.

"We can't! The door's locked! And nobody heard me yelling."

Ned did not answer. He grabbed the new extinguisher, which was more effective, and played it on the flames. Nancy sprayed a stream with the one he had used. Finally the blaze began to die down.

The couple started looking for another exit but there was none. As they went up the smoke-filled stairway, the door to the corridor suddenly opened. There were exclamations of dismay from above.

"There's a fire in the prop room!" a man exclaimed. "Call the fire department! Quick! Call the police!"

Nancy and Ned scooted up and explained to them what had happened.

"You put out the fire?" a girl asked unbelievingly. "Why, it's Nancy Drew! Oh, I think you're wonderful! I could never be that brave!"

"This is my friend Ned Nickerson," Nancy said. "He discovered the fire and should get the credit."

Other members of the cast and the director now crowded around the couple and demanded to hear the whole story. Nancy and Ned quickly explained, then asked who had locked the door to the basement. Everyone denied having done it, or having been downstairs.

"I'm sure," said Nancy, "that the fire was set deliberately."

"What!" Mr. Skank cried out.

By this time firemen and police had arrived. After an examination of the prop room, they agreed that the fire was of an incendiary nature. Someone had deliberately placed costumes in a heap on the floor, oil-soaked them, and started the blaze.

"How wicked!" a young woman cried out.

Nancy and Ned had been whispering about the possibility that the pudgy man might have been the one who had done it. They speculated that possibly he had sneaked into the building while the actors and actresses were arriving. The couple queried each one in the cast, but none of them had seen anyone who fitted that description.

"We have no leads at all," Nancy said, disappointed.

"One may turn up," Ned replied. "The police will probably find something."

The firemen and police were sure that the arsonist had escaped. Nevertheless, each classroom was thoroughly searched. But they found no one.

One officer said, "What I'd like to know is his motive for starting the fire. It's rather farfetched, but it is possible that someone who was turned down for a part in the play became disgruntled and wanted revenge. Mr. Skank, do you by any chance know of such a person?"

"No," the director answered quickly. "But I understand there's a gang of firebugs around here. I'm inclined to think those bad boys are responsible."

By this time the odor from the smoke had permeated the stage. Between this unpleasantness and the fact that many of the players were upset by the unfortunate affair, the director dismissed them all for the night.

"I'm glad to go," Nancy said to Ned. "I couldn't possibly have rehearsed my part. All I want to do is get home and shampoo my hair. It smells of smoke and my clothes do too."

Then she changed the subject. "If the arsonist was Gus, why do you think he did it? And why did he take such drastic measures?"

Ned reminded Nancy that a person with Gus's reputation was unpredictable.

"He could be capable of almost anything. It's my guess he's trying to harm you or me, Nancy, so you won't be able to continue with the case. Then he'd be free to carry on his tapping without interruption."

Nancy frowned. "You mean he would go so far as to hope you'd run downstairs to the fire and I'd follow? If we didn't, he'd let the fire eat up through the stage and maybe harm people?"

"Who knows what that idiot had in mind?" Ned remarked angrily.

"Do you think he locked the door?"

"Yes."

When they reached the Drew house, Nancy's father was just driving in from a meeting he had attended. He was amazed that the rehearsal was over so early, but even more amazed when he heard the reason for it.

"I don't like what's going on," Mr. Drew said. "By the way, I have learned nothing more about Gus Woonton or his parents or the whereabouts of any of them."

Nancy suggested that they look through Gus's diary to see if they could find any clues. She brought the book down from her bedroom and the three took turns reading from it while they ate some cookies and Coke Nancy had brought in.

"I'd say Gus is lucky to be out of prison," Ned remarked, after reading several items. "Man, the things he pulled, even as a kid!"

Mr. Drew nodded. "I don't see how his parents stood it. And Gus was pretty cool about it all. Listen to this item:

'August 28—We're still at the Grand Hotel and everybody in it bores me. This morning I sneaked off before breakfast and helped myself to a motorboat. Boy, did I have fun! Scared a lot of people on the lake half out of their wits. I pulled in near a dock where I saw a man's clothes. Guess he'd gone swimming. And there was a wallet; just waiting for me to take it!'

"I'd say the guy is an egomaniac," the lawyer added.

The last notation in the diary, Mr. Drew pointed out, had been written four years before on the day Gus had been taken to the Beverly. This puzzled Nancy. If Gus had recently visited his old home, why hadn't he written this in his diary?

"Maybe it's a friend of Gus's who comes there," she said. "Dad, would you find out from the Beverly whether Gus had a pal who might have left there about the same time he did?"

"I'll do it tomorrow," her father promised.

Ned said he must leave. "Nancy, if you don't need my car any more, I'll take it."

"All right. I guess there's no use in my trying to fool anyone."

The following morning Nancy hurried down to the kitchen to prepare her father's breakfast. While the oatmeal was cooking, Nancy decided to check a couple of items in the diary. She had put it on a table in the living room.

"Why, it's gone!" Nancy exclaimed when she saw the book was not on the table.

After a moment's thought she decided that her father probably had taken it upstairs when he went to bed. But a few minutes later, when he came down to breakfast, Mr. Drew said he had not carried it to his room.

"I didn't touch it."

Father and daughter stared at each other for several seconds. "It must have been stolen!" Nancy said slowly.

The Drews quickly checked doors and windows. All were locked and chains on the front and back doors were in place. Nothing else had been taken.

"Someone got in here somehow," the lawyer said, setting his jaw firmly.

Puzzled, Nancy and her father ran upstairs. The only windows which were open were those in their bedrooms. The Drews could find no evidence on any of them that an intruder had entered the house. The screens were locked in place and there were no holes in them. Furthermore, no personal property had been removed.

Nancy hurried to the third floor, followed by her father. Certainly someone had gained access to the house.

Nancy said, "Since the intruder wanted the diary, it's apparent he was Gus or a friend of his."

"It looks that way," Mr. Drew agreed.

No burglar was in sight but a window at the far end of the attic was wide open. There was no screen in it.

"We never leave that window open," said Nancy.

"But only a human fly could climb up here on the outside!" Mr. Drew declared.

CHAPTER IX

Suspicious Salesman

As Nancy hurried to the open attic window, she wondered if someone might be clinging to the sill and trying to hide. There were no fingers showing and cautiously she looked out.

"See anything?" Mr. Drew asked, joining her.

"Nobody in sight," Nancy replied. "But, Dad, look! Here's a natural ladder."

She pointed to a stout trellis which ran from the ground to the roof.

"A lot of those leaves have been torn off," Nancy said. "I guess the intruder came up this way."

"He's still a human fly," her father remarked. "The man could have fallen and broken his neck. He must be mighty sure of himself to have attempted such a climb."

A thought came to Nancy's mind. "Dad, it

never occurred to me to look for a trellis at Miss Carter's. Maybe the tapper gets into her attic that way."

"Let me know what you find," the lawyer said.

Before leaving for his office, Mr. Drew decided to board up the attic window. He found a piece of wood in the garage and soon had it in place.

"I'm glad you did that instead of ripping the vines off the house," Nancy said as they ate breakfast. "The ivy looks so pretty."

Later, as she was clearing the table, Nancy realized that actually she was not very safe from her pursuer. Despite all her precautions, he knew she had brought the diary home. That meant the tapper or someone else who slept in the secret room had discovered that the diary was missing.

"I still have that cupboard key in my purse," Nancy reminded herself. "Someone may try to snatch it."

She decided to put the key on a ribbon and hang it around her neck. An hour later, with warnings from her father still ringing in her ears, Nancy drove away. She locked herself in the convertible and turned on the air conditioner. As she rode along, Nancy began to feel easier. No one seemed to be following her.

Upon arriving at Miss Carter's, Nancy parked the car in the driveway and then walked all the way around the house. No vines were growing on it and there was nothing else to which a person might cling in order to climb any of the walls.

"Well, there goes my theory about the human fly," she thought. "But *how* does that tapper get into the house?"

She found Miss Carter and Hannah Gruen very upset. Five more cats had been stolen during the night!

"The garage was securely locked," the actress said. "Someone has a skeleton key, that's sure. I must have a padlock put on the door. Fortunately my little beauties that are to go to the show had been brought into the house—I wanted to help with the grooming—so they weren't taken."

"Did you call the police?" Nancy asked.

"Oh, yes," Miss Carter answered. "Detective Keely came. He made a thorough search of the grounds and came up with one good clue."

"What was that?"

"The thief was a short, stocky man who wore spiked golf shoes. There were holes in the ground outside the garage but not inside it," Miss Carter went on. "Maybe the thief took off his shoes before he went in for the cats, but in any case you couldn't detect the marks in the hay."

Nancy asked where the footprints led and learned they crossed the neighbor's back yard and went out to the street.

The conversation was interrupted by the ringing of the doorbell. Nancy offered to go downstairs and answer it. To her surprise Bess and George stood there. They had borrowed the Marvin car.

"Hi!" they both said, and Bess added, "You didn't expect us to get back in time for the cat show, did you?"

George grinned. "What's more, we just couldn't stay away from the mystery any longer. We didn't pick up any clues, though, to Gus Woonton."

"Girls," said Nancy, "the cat thief was here last night and took five more Persians."

"Oh, no!" Bess cried out.

"See what happens when we're not here to guard the garage?" George remarked.

Bess looked sober. Hesitatingly she confessed that on the drive to Berryville she had told George she would not sleep in the garage another night.

"But I guess I'll have to change my mind," Bess said. "I'm terribly sorry to hear about the theft."

"Fortunately the cats to be sold at the cat show today were in the house," Nancy told her chums.

The three girls went upstairs. "I'm delighted you're back," said Miss Carter. Upon learning that the cousins would take up their vigil in the garage that evening, she added, "You're dolls, both of you."

Presently Nancy said, "I suppose we should start soon for the cat show. How many miles is it to South Bedford, Miss Carter?"

"I'd say about twenty."

Hannah Gruen offered to pack a lunch for the girls and went down to the kitchen.

During the next hour Miss Carter directed the preparations for the trip to the show. Five carrying cases were brought into the house. Brushes, eyewash, a bottle of delicately perfumed spray and cans of cat food were packed in a large tote bag. George placed the bag in Nancy's car and also a sack of kitty litter.

"And don't forget to take a jug of water and a dish," Miss Carter said. "Oh dear! I wish so much that I might be there. I hope you have no trouble selling the cats because I really need the money. Oh yes! One more thing. Be sure to put in several paper hankies so you can keep my cats' mouths and feet immaculately clean."

Out of sight of Miss Carter, George grinned and whispered to the other girls, "We always have cats at my house. They certainly never get all this attention. They keep themselves groomed!"

Bess giggled. "Mine do too. But then, you and I aren't in the business of selling cats."

"Correction," said George. "Today we are."

By this time the girls' lunch was ready. It was put into the car and with wishes of good luck from Hannah, Nancy and the cousins rode off.

When they reached the South Bedford municipal auditorium where the cat show was being held, the girls carried the Persians inside. Nancy stopped at the desk to claim the booth Miss Carter had reserved.

"You have number ten," the man told Nancy. "As you enter, keep to your right. You'll find it easily."

As soon as the cages had been set in place and doors between them opened so the cats might roam around, the girls tacked up a large sign to an overhead beam. It read:

CARTER'S CATS
LOVABLE COMPANIONABLE DECORATIVE
PUREBRED PERSIANS

Visitors to the show began to stop and admire Miss Carter's cats.

"They're perfectly beautiful!" one woman exclaimed. "I wish I could buy one, but I travel a great deal and couldn't take care of it."

A couple stopped. The woman said to the man, "Oh, Claude dear, I'd love to have one of these. What do you say?"

"Nothing doing," he answered rather roughly. "Those long haired cats get hairs all over the place." He took the woman's arm and pulled her away from the booth.

Bess sighed. "At this rate maybe we'll have to take all these cats back home."

"Don't be discouraged," Nancy said. "We've been here only fifteen minutes."

At that moment three judges—two women and a man—walked up and carefully examined Miss Carter's Persians. A few moments later they went off to confer, then returned, smiling. One of the women placed the "Best in Show" ribbon on Abatha's cage.

"How wonderful!" Bess exclaimed.

The other woman put a first-place blue ribbon on Rosemond. All the other cats received second-place red awards.

"Congratulations," said the third judge. "I'm sorry Miss Carter couldn't be here. Give her my regards—I'm Craig Kendall."

"I will," said Nancy. "This will make her very happy."

After the judges walked away, George suggested the price of the cats be raised, with Abatha having the highest amount. Nancy and Bess agreed.

Many passers-by stopped to praise the beauty of the Persians. One woman asked the price of each. Nancy told her.

"Oh," she said, "that's rather high, isn't it? A man on the other side of the show is selling Persians much cheaper."

The three girls were interested and a trifle suspicious. George asked the number of the seller's booth.

"It's number thirty," the woman replied. "I

remember because I told the man I might be back."

George told Nancy and Bess she was going over to see the Persian cats, and hurried off. When she returned several minutes later, George was very excited.

"Girls," she exclaimed, "I'm sure that the five Persian cats in booth thirty are some that were stolen from Miss Carter!"

CHAPTER X

Precarious Climb

AT George's announcement Nancy and Bess caught their breath. They were sure George was right and decided to look at the Persian cats.

"I found out," she went on, "that the man had ten, but he has sold five."

"Nancy," said Bess, "you go with George. I'll stay here with our cats."

The other two hurried off, but as they neared booth thirty, Nancy held George back.

"Don't you think it would be better if we pretend to be strolling casually and stop to look at the cats?"

"I suppose you're right," George agreed.

The girls slowed to a leisurely pace. As they passed the booth, Nancy was sure the cats were Miss Carter's stolen Persians. They looked exactly the same as the ones the girls were selling.

Nancy studied the man who was in charge. He

was short and rather stocky. Was he the one who had worn the spiked golf shoes?

George spoke to the man. "You have some beautiful cats here. I saw them a few minutes ago and went to get my friend. She's crazy about Persians."

"Yes, I am," said Nancy. She asked the price. When he named it, she said, "Why, that's cheap for such fine animals. They're pedigreed, of course?"

"Oh sure," the man replied.

"Do you have the pedigree papers with you?" Nancy asked.

The man hesitated for a few seconds, then said, "They're here some place. You buy one of the cats and leave your name and address. I'll send you the pedigree later."

Nancy smiled at him. "But I want to see the pedigree before I buy."

The man's attitude changed. "If you don't want to buy on my say-so, don't," he said. "Next customer?" He turned away from the girls, ignoring them completely.

They walked off. "Nancy, what do you think?" George asked.

"I strongly suspect he's a phony. It wouldn't hurt to call the police. If the man has nothing to hide, he won't be in trouble. But if he's the thief—"

Nancy stopped at a nearby phone booth and put in the call. The sergeant on duty said two men would be sent to the cat show at once. He instructed Nancy to wait for them at the Carter booth so she could go with the officers to point out the suspect.

"I wonder if Bess sold any cats," said George as the girls went on. As they neared booth ten, they saw only four cats.

Bess greeted them with a giggle. "Want to know who the real salesman is around here?" she asked, thumping her chest.

"Congratulations," said Nancy. Then she told Bess about the man in booth thirty and said the police would be arriving in a few minutes to talk to him.

Bess gave Nancy a long look and shook her head. "Everywhere you go there's excitement."

Nancy laughed. "This may not end up being exciting at all. Here come two men now. I wonder if they're plainclothesmen from the police department, or potential customers."

The men stopped at the booth.

"Miss Drew?" one of them asked.

When Nancy acknowledged her identity, the two men opened their coats and showed police detective badges. They requested her to point out the suspect to them. Bess asked to go along.

"George, see if you can sell a cat while I'm gone," she teased.

Nancy led the way toward booth thirty. As they

approached it, she gasped. The man and all the cats were gone!

"He isn't here!" she exclaimed, embarrassed.

The group stood in front of the empty booth, mystified. Nancy was sure that the detectives felt that a hoax had been pulled on them.

"Are you sure this is the right place?" one of them asked Nancy.

"Oh, yes."

"Now listen, young lady!" the other officer said. "Don't you know it's a serious offense to bring out the police on a wild-goose chase like this?"

Bess was aghast. She said quickly, "Nancy has done nothing wrong. She's an amateur detective and we've been trying to trace cats that were stolen from a woman we know. Her name's Carter."

The taller of the two men looked at Nancy. "Amateur detective, eh?" He scoffed. "Well, if there's one thing in this world I have no use for it's an amateur detective."

Nancy was stung by the remark. Somehow she must prove to these men that she was not faking. She saw a woman in booth thirty-one who was busy grooming some Maltese cats. She dashed over and touched her arm.

"Pardon me, but could you tell us where the man went who had the cats in booth thirty?"

"I can't tell you where he went," the woman

answered, "but I can tell you this: after you and the other young lady left here, he began to act strange. He mumbled to himself and then called out to passers-by:

" 'Want to buy a cat cheap?' The price was so ridiculous, he sold them all in a couple of minutes. Then he rushed out of here as if a cyclone were chasing him."

Nancy was so appreciative of the woman's assistance she could have kissed her. But she merely said:

"I suspect that the cats the man was selling had been stolen from a home where I'm staying. I called the police and here are two detectives. They doubted my story, so I am very grateful to you for helping me out."

The woman turned to the detectives. "Everything I've just said is true. Besides, I can easily believe that the man is a thief. He acted very odd right from the beginning—shifty-eyed and sort of scared—and wouldn't let the judges look at his Persians. Even the cats didn't seem to like him. He was having a hard time with them."

The taller detective turned to Nancy. "I'm sorry I thought you were kidding us." Then he quickly defended himself. "The police get so many phony calls I guess we're kind of rough on people sometimes."

He then asked for a full description of the suspect. The woman in booth thirty-one gave a clear picture of the man.

"Short and kind of stocky. He walked with quick steps. As I said he was shifty-eyed and acted nervous. He had dark hair and eyes. I guess that's all I can tell you about him."

The detective said she had been a great help and they would try to locate the man. The detectives said good-by to everyone and left. After Nancy had thanked the woman again, she and Bess hurried back to their own booth.

"I'm sorry I didn't get a look at that man's Persian cats," Bess said. "He probably took the list of the purchasers so there's no chance of tracing him or the cats."

"I'm afraid not," Nancy agreed. "Let's just hope they found good homes."

The girls were delighted that George had sold two cats and within a few minutes Nancy sold one. By now the crowd had dwindled and it was approaching closing time.

"Oh dear!" said Bess. "Do you suppose we'll have to take Abatha back home? Miss Carter needs the money and will be disappointed that we didn't sell all the Persians. Should we lower the price?"

"I don't want to do that," said Nancy.

She took the Persian from its cage and fondled the fluffy animal. Maybe her gesture would appeal to some prospective buyer!

Among the people who stopped at the booth was a little boy. His pockets were stuffed with boxes of popcorn and candy. In one hand he carried a curled-up paper whistle.

He walked close to the cat and gave a great blow on the whistle. Not only did it make a loud noise but the curled-up section flew out at the little animal and hit it in the face.

"Oh, you naughty boy!" Nancy cried as the cat leaped from her arms.

To her dismay, it scooted up a post and onto a crossbeam. She turned toward the cat and held up one hand.

"Don't be frightened," she said soothingly. "I won't let him do it again. Please come down."

The cat paid no attention, so Nancy climbed up on a chair and reached for it. But the cat scooted farther away and climbed high onto a rafter of the auditorium.

"Oh dear!" said Bess. "What are we going to do now?"

Nancy continued to cajole the Persian to climb down, but without success. Bess and George tried persuading the cat to come back, but they had no luck either.

"There's only one thing left to do," said Nancy. "I'm glad I wore pants."

She caught the beam above, hoisted herself onto it, and walked along it to the rafter. Then she began climbing toward the cat.

"Oh, Nancy," Bess wailed, "please come back!"

"Oh, Nancy," wailed Bess, "that's too dangerous! The cat isn't worth it. Please come back."

Nancy assured Bess she would be all right and continued to climb. Onlookers began to gather and offer all kinds of advice. Most of the men urged Nancy to go on but to be careful. The women begged her to come down.

Bess had turned her back on the scene. She was ashen. Her lips were moving and George assumed she was praying for Nancy's safe return.

The cat watched Nancy from a high beam. As the girl finally reached the beam on which the animal stood, she straddled it and started to inch her way along.

"Come, pussy," she coaxed. "Nobody's going to hurt you."

The cat waited a moment. Then, instead of coming toward Nancy, it went the other way.

"Oh, you meanie!" Nancy exclaimed.

The crowd below watched tensely. Finally one of the men called to her.

"Hang on! I'll toss a net up and you can catch the animal that way."

The man dashed off. He came back in a couple of minutes with a fish net, which he threw upward. It did not reach the beam. Once more he gave the net a mighty heave. Still it did not reach Nancy.

"I guess it's no use," she called down.

A very tall man among the onlookers offered to try his luck. He rolled the net into a ball and gave a mighty heave. Nancy reached down to grab the net and caught it.

But the weight of the net and her sudden shift in position caused Nancy to lose her balance!

CHAPTER XI

Bess Plays Cupid

As Nancy slipped from the high beam, people below gasped, others screamed.

"Oh no, no!" George cried.

Nancy herself had been terrified for a fraction of a second. In a desperate attempt to save herself, she clung tightly to the beam by one arm. Then, with great effort, she swung her right leg over the beam and gradually pulled herself to an upright position.

"Bravo! Bravo!" cried several of the men below her and began to clap.

"Yea! Yea!" shouted several relieved children.

All this time Nancy had managed to hold onto the net. Now she unrolled it, and with a well-placed aim, finally snared the Persian. Its protests at being made a prisoner almost caused Nancy to lose her balance again.

There were gasps of dismay from the watching crowd and a flash bulb went off. Nancy looked down. A photographer had snapped her picture!

"Oh dear!" she thought. "This whole adventure has been such a mess."

The cat had quieted down and now Nancy inched her way backward, pulling the animal along. Slowly she shinned down the rafter to the crossbeam.

"Bess! George! Will you catch the cat?" Nancy requested.

"Yes. Let it go," George replied.

Besides the girls' outstretched arms there were several other willing hands. Nancy dropped the net containing the animal. The Persian was immediately put back into its cage, and Nancy came down the rest of the way safely. The watchers showered her with congratulations.

"Thanks a lot," she said, blushing. All she wanted to do now was to get back to Berryville.

A voice from among the onlookers called out, "I'll buy the cat! I like spunky animals. How much is it?"

Before Nancy could answer, George spoke up. "The price is higher now."

People laughed and the man called out, "You mean the higher the cat, the higher the price?"

"Exactly," George said. "How about our having an auction? We'll start with the original price and go up from there."

Nancy was amused and wondered if the scheme would work.

"I'll pay exactly the figure you named," a woman said.

"And I'll give you twenty-five dollars more," a man called out.

"Anyone bid twenty-five more, twenty-five more?" said George, who began to enjoy her role as auctioneer.

As the bidding went on, Nancy and Bess became more and more astounded. The Persian cat finally sold for over three times what the original price had been!

When Nancy mentioned to Bess that she wondered if this had been the right thing to do, her chum said quickly, "I thought all along the price for a prize cat was too low. Besides, Miss Carter can certainly use the money."

The girls said good-by to the lovely Persian which was now resting comfortably in the arms of a teen-age girl whose father had purchased it for her.

She smiled at the girls. "I just love my new pet."

"I'm so glad you do," Nancy said. "Be kind to Abatha."

At that moment the young man who had taken her picture said, "I want it for our local paper. Quite a story. Please tell me your name and address."

Nancy did not relish this publicity but did not see how she could avoid it. She identified herself.

"You're from River Heights?" the photographer asked. "Are you related to the famous lawyer Carson Drew?"

Bess answered the question. "She certainly is and she does a lot of detective work in connection with her father's cases."

Nancy was embarrassed, but the photographer beamed. "This will make a cool story," he said, putting away his notebook and starting off. "I can't wait to get it in the paper."

When the girls reached Miss Carter's home, they found that Mrs. Bealing had returned from River Heights. At once she said to Nancy, "I hope you're not too tired to drive me downtown. I must buy some food."

Nancy said she would be glad to take the nurse as soon as she had a chance to freshen up and change her clothes. The three girls went upstairs to Miss Carter's room. Hannah Gruen was talking to the actress.

Proudly Nancy opened her purse and took out a large wad of bills. "We sold every cat," she announced.

"That's marvelous!" Miss Carter exclaimed. "You girls are wonderful—why, Nancy, you've given me too much money!"

The three "salesmen" giggled. "No, I haven't,"

Nancy said, and then told the story of George auctioning off the last cat. Both women laughed. "Good work," said Hannah.

Bess spoke up. "It was all because Nancy climbed into the rafters to get the cat and twice she nearly fell off—"

"Oh my goodness!" Hannah Gruen cried out.

Nancy smiled. "Don't worry. I'm still in one piece."

Miss Carter shook her head. "I appreciate all this," she said, "but, Nancy, you shouldn't have taken the chance." Then she chuckled. "You must be as lithe as a kitten yourself!"

While Bess and George told her about the strange man with the cats at the show, Nancy took a quick shower and changed her clothes. Then she and Mrs. Bealing set off for the shopping center of Berryville.

As they entered the parking lot, the nurse suddenly exclaimed, "Nancy, there's the man who was looking for Miss Violette!"

"Where?"

Mrs. Bealing pointed him out. He had parked his red convertible and was now hurrying out to Main Street. Nancy dashed after the tall, handsome man and in a few moments caught up to him.

"Pardon me," she said, walking beside him, "but are you Mr. Toby Simpson?"

He looked at her in amazement, then said with a smile, "Yes, I am."

"You don't know me," Nancy said. "My name is Nancy Drew and I'm staying with the woman you call Miss Violette."

The actor stopped walking and stared at Nancy. "But how did you know—?"

"I don't blame you for being surprised," Nancy said, then quickly explained that Miss Carter had found out he had come to the house asking for Miss Violette.

By this time Mrs. Bealing had caught up to them, and Nancy introduced her. The actor smiled. "You're the woman who came to the door when I rang and said Miss Violette did not live there."

"That's right. I never heard Miss Carter's stage name."

Mr. Simpson said that back in the days when he had been in plays with her, she had insisted that no one call her by any name except Miss Violette. He had assumed that she had continued the custom.

An idea came to Nancy. She said to the actor, "If you're not busy this evening, I think it would be fun if you came to dinner at the house. We could let it be a complete surprise to Miss Carter."

The man's eyes lighted up. "I can't think of anything I'd rather do," he replied. "What time would you like me to get there?"

"Would seven o'clock be all right?" It occurred

to Nancy that even if they had a simple dinner not much time was being allowed for its preparation.

"Seven o'clock will be fine. I'll be there and thank you very much."

"Then good-by for now," said Nancy.

She and Mrs. Bealing hurried off to the market. "This is very exciting," the nurse said. "Now all we need is to have the tapper show up and spoil the show. I can't understand why the police haven't rounded up somebody in this case. Well, what do you think we should have for dinner?"

"Steak is always safe," Nancy replied. "And how about a lemon meringue pie? I'll telephone Hannah and ask if she'll make one right away."

She dashed off to a street phone while Mrs. Bealing started to shop. It was nearly six o'clock by the time they reached home.

Bess, intrigued by the thought of a romantic meeting between Miss Violette and Toby Simpson, found it hard not to give away the secret. She and George had set the table. Flowers and candles gave it a very festive air. Hannah Gruen was just putting the meringue on the pie. She had also made a tasty-looking tossed salad with tomatoes and cucumbers.

"We'll start with melon," Nancy announced. "Then will come the steak, French fries, and string beans. Everybody can help prepare them for cooking."

Bess had gone upstairs and suggested that Miss Carter wear one of her most becoming dresses. "And I'll comb your hair in a modern style," she offered.

"What's going on?" the actress asked, a suspicious look coming into her eyes.

Bess did not answer directly. She said, "Don't you think we should celebrate selling all those cats and Nancy rescuing the last one?"

Miss Carter smiled. "I suppose we should." She pointed out a filmy pale-blue dress and Bess helped her put it on.

"You look darling," the girl said. Then she started working on the actress's fluffy gray hair. Within a few minutes Miss Carter's long hair was arranged in an attractive style.

As she looked in the mirror, the woman smiled. "I do look lovely, don't I?" A faraway expression came over her face. "Like I used to be when I played in *The Dancer and the Fool.*"

Presently George came upstairs and together the two girls carried Miss Carter to the first floor. They had dimmed the lights in the dining room so she would not notice the extra place at the table. The girls sat down in the living room with her, while Mrs. Bealing and Hannah Gruen were putting the finishing touches on the meal.

At exactly seven o'clock the front doorbell rang. Nancy went to answer, followed by Bess and George. They had already decided that the meeting between Miss Carter and Mr. Simpson should take place alone in the living room.

When Nancy opened the door, she put one finger to her lips and merely said, "Won't you come in?"

Mr. Simpson, smiling, stepped into the hall. Nancy pointed out the doorway to the living room and motioned for him to go inside. The girls huddled together, waiting.

The next moment they heard a cry of delight from Miss Violette. "Toby! Toby! You've come back to me!"

"Yes, dear. It has been so many years. I lost complete track of you, but today I had a little luck, and thanks to your friend Nancy Drew, here I am."

There was a long silence and the girls figured the couple were having a loving embrace. A few minutes later Miss Carter called the girls inside.

She formally introduced Mr. Simpson, then asked for a complete explanation of the whole affair. Nancy quickly told the story, then the three girls said they must go out to the kitchen to help.

On the way, Bess whispered excitedly, "I'm so happy I could just burst!"

"I feel pretty good about the whole thing myself," George said.

When the girls entered the kitchen, Hannah and Mrs. Bealing wanted to know about the meeting between the actress and actor. When they heard it had been a happy one, both were pleased.

A little later, when everyone was seated at the table and grace had been said, Miss Carter told the others a little about her early life on the stage.

"Then finally I played opposite Toby and we began to date," she explained.

The actor had not taken his eyes from the woman and now he said, "I played the part of the fool in the story for so long I guess I just lived the part in my everyday life. In any case I was a fool to think my work was more important than marrying my leading lady."

Bess had been touched by the story and the meeting. Now she looked directly at the couple and said, "It's not too late!"

Her remark was so unexpected that there was dead silence for several seconds. Bess, embarrassed, apologized profusely, but Toby smiled at her gratefully.

"You have said the very thing I wanted to," he told her and looked lovingly at Miss Carter. "As soon as you are well again, what say we try it?"

Everyone waited anxiously for her answer. Taking Toby Simpson's hand and kissing him on the cheek, she said, "I'll try it if you think I can be of help to you."

"Oh, you can!"

Now there was real rejoicing. Everyone was so excited it was hard to settle down to the dinner in front of them.

But after a while the conversation got around to the reason Nancy and her friends had come to Miss Carter's house. Toby Simpson wanted to hear the story in detail. When Nancy revealed the fact that she suspected a young man named Gus Woonton, Mr. Simpson frowned.

"I once met a couple named Woonton," he said. "I believe they had a son Gus."

CHAPTER XII

"Try to Catch Me!"

AT Mr. Simpson's announcement all eyes turned in his direction, and there were gasps of astonishment.

"You actually met Gus Woonton's parents?" Nancy asked.

The actor smiled. "*A* Gus Woonton. He may not be the person you're looking for."

"Oh, I'm sure he is!" Bess said excitedly.

George remarked, "It's a rather uncommon name. Where did Mr. and Mrs. Woonton say their son is?"

"They didn't say."

Hannah Gruen spoke up. "That's not surprising, if he was a problem child. It isn't exactly a subject they'd be likely to talk about to strangers."

George asked, "Where do Mr. and Mrs. Woonton live now?"

The actor shook his head, saying he had met them in St. Louis about four years before but had never seen them again.

"I heard through some friends of mine I knew in the theater that both the Woontons had passed away."

"Poor Gus," said Nancy. After a moment she added, "Mr. Simpson, have you any idea when this happened and where?"

"Sorry, but I haven't. If it will help you, I might try to track down some information through those same friends."

Nancy thanked him but suggested that he not bother until after she had talked with her father.

"Perhaps he can find out. St. Louis is a good lead."

"I understand," the actor went on, "that the Woontons I met had a great deal of money in savings accounts and securities. This fact should help you in tracking down the couple."

Nancy smiled. "It's a very good clue, Mr. Simpson. I'll phone my father in a little while and tell him."

Dinner was over a short time later. By tacit arrangement Miss Carter and Mr. Simpson were left alone in the living room. Mrs. Bealing and Hannah went into the kitchen, while Bess and George carried out the empty dishes from the table.

Nancy telephoned her father who was amazed

at the progress she had made on the case. He promised to call the Beverly immediately and to let Nancy know what he found out.

"I can't wait to hear," she said.

In about an hour Mr. Drew telephoned his findings. He said that the owner of the Beverly, Dr. Norton Jones, had been astonished to learn that Mr. and Mrs. Woonton had passed away.

"Dr. Jones told me," the lawyer went on, "that no checks for services to Gus had come for several months before the young man had run away. The owner had not been surprised at this. He had assumed Gus's parents were on a long trip and would eventually pay.

"He was amazed when I told him what we suspect about Gus, saying the Beverly had tried without success to find him. The doctor had thought possibly Gus knew where his parents were and had gone to them."

Nancy and her father talked for a long time, speculating on whether Gus had flown to St. Louis or some other place to claim the money which probably had been left to him.

"If he did," Nancy said, "why would he have come back here? Dad, I think perhaps Gus doesn't know his parents have passed away. He couldn't find them, and since this house is his true home, he came here."

"Perhaps," the lawyer said. "I'll make inquiries

in St. Louis tomorrow morning. I hope I can turn up some worthwhile information for you, Nancy. And now I'll say good night. Sweet dreams."

"And to you too, Dad."

As Nancy put down the phone, Mr. Simpson carrying Miss Carter came into the hall.

He laughed gaily and said, "I thought I'd bring my bride-to-be to her room. Also, I wanted to say good night to the rest of you."

Nancy and the others accompanied the couple to Miss Carter's room, where they all chatted for a while. The actor declared this was the most delightful evening he had spent in a long time and promised to return soon.

"I'll be waiting," Miss Carter told him with a happy laugh.

After he had gone, Mrs. Bealing and Hannah Gruen went around to check all windows and doors on the first floor. They were securely locked. The lights were turned off and everyone went to bed.

Nancy found it difficult to sleep. She turned from side to side, trying to put the mystery out of her mind, but found this impossible. Suddenly she became aware of tapping sounds. Nancy was not sure of their location but thought they were coming from the first floor.

"If that's the mysterious tapper back again," she thought, "how did he enter the house? Apparently he had sneaked in after the police had made their round. Maybe I can get a message across to him."

Nancy quickly put on her robe and the tap shoes which she had brought with her. She tiptoed into the hall and listened.

The tapping sound was indeed coming from the first floor. Slowly and quietly Nancy descended the front stairway. By this time she knew the house so well she could make her way in the dark.

Her heart thumping, Nancy traced the sounds. They were coming from under the dining-room floor. She tiptoed to the spot. The staccato noises were definitely not in code, but did resemble the sounds of tap dancing. What should she do now?

"I'd better not go into the basement alone," Nancy decided. "Perhaps I should run upstairs and wake the others."

Then, to her amazement, the tapping sounds began to come in Morse code. The message was, "Try to catch me!"

"Who are you?" Nancy tapped back. There was no answer.

On a sudden hunch she sent a message of her own. "If you are Gus Woonton, I have some very valuable information for you."

There was complete silence. Had the mysterious intruder fled?

Nancy's loud tapping had aroused the sleepers

upstairs. All of them except Miss Carter came rushing down, turning on lights.

"Nancy!" Bess cried out. "What's going on? Why didn't you call us?"

"I'll explain later," Nancy replied. "Right now we have a good chance to solve the mystery! Divide up and look outdoors and all through the house for the tapper. George, will you come to the basement with me?"

As the others scattered, the two girls unlocked the door to the basement and hurried down the steps. George had snapped on the light as they descended and now she and Nancy gazed around them. They saw no one. Windows and the outside door were locked.

"Where could the tapper have gone?" George asked, puzzled. "The only other opening we know of leads to the secret room. Let's look in there."

Nancy got the hook and the panel was yanked open. The secret room was vacant. The two girls made a minute search of the walls but found no sign of another concealed opening. Then they tested the ceiling and finally searched the floor for a trap door to a subcellar. Their efforts were futile.

George frowned. "This is impossible."

Nancy went out to the big room and sat down to think. She was certain there must be another opening into the basement.

George came to stand in front of her friend.

"Let's face it. The tapper is really cool. Why don't we forget him and just try to find out why he was tapping?"

Nancy stood up and said she would get the small stepladder from the kitchen. She was back in a couple of minutes and set it under the spot from where the tapping had come.

George, meanwhile, had found a hammer. She handed it to Nancy who began to tap for hollow places in the ceiling.

"There are a lot of deep dents in the wood," she remarked, "but I don't hear any hollow sounds."

"Probably," said George, "the man was tapping to attract your attention and just goading you on to hunt for him."

"But why?" Nancy asked.

"That's a good question," George replied.

Nancy moved the stepladder a few feet and tapped again on the ceiling. In a moment her eyes lighted up. "George, I've found something!"

George held the flashlight toward the spot. "See any opening or cracks?" she asked hopefully.

"No, but I think this beam moves. Climb up here with me and see if we can budge it."

The two girls pushed and pulled on the beam.

"Is it my imagination," George said presently, "or did this move a teeny bit?"

"I think it did," Nancy replied. "Let's pull harder."

Nancy and George tugged so hard that both of them lost their balance and were forced to jump to the floor. Before they had a chance to climb the ladder again, they were interrupted by Bess. She called down frantically from the top of the stairway.

"Come here quick!"

Nancy and George dashed to the kitchen. Bess was already running out the back door. The other girls followed.

"What's up?" George queried.

Bess pointed. Mrs. Bealing and Hannah Gruen were bending over an unconscious man, who was face down in the driveway!

CHAPTER XIII

Empty!

GENTLY the women turned the man over onto his back. Nancy and the others gasped.

"He's Fred Bunce!" Bess exclaimed. "Oh, I hope he's not badly hurt!"

"We'd better call Mrs. Bunce," Nancy said at once.

She hurried to the back door and rang the bell. There was no answer and Nancy began to worry that something might have happened to Mrs. Bunce also.

"But perhaps she's only a heavy sleeper," Nancy told herself, and pounded more loudly than before. In a moment Mrs. Bunce looked out a second-floor window.

"Who's there?" she asked. "What's the idea of waking people in the middle of the night?"

Quickly Nancy explained about her husband.

The woman gasped and said she would be right down. When she saw Mr. Bunce lying in the driveway, she began to cry loudly and wring her hands.

"Oh, he's dead! Somebody's killed him!" she shrieked.

Hannah Gruen spoke up. "Your husband isn't dead. He's just unconscious. I think we'd better carry him into the house, and if he doesn't revive soon, we'll call a doctor."

In the meantime Mrs. Bealing had made a cursory examination and said that the victim had a swelling on the back of his head.

"He either fell or something hit him," she declared.

To herself Nancy said, "Or *somebody* hit him."

She noticed that Mr. Bunce was fully dressed. Had he been out and just returning home?

"And why," thought Nancy, "is he in Miss Carter's driveway?"

As Bess and George carried the unconscious man into the Bunces's living room and laid him on the couch, Nancy said to his wife, "I'm sure your husband will be all right. Tell me, why did he go outside?"

"I don't know. He went to bed when I did and I didn't hear him get up."

"What was his reason for getting fully dressed?" Nancy asked herself.

Mrs. Bealing and Hannah Gruen gave the man

first-aid, while his wife paced up and down the living room muttering to herself and sobbing.

"Do you want to call your doctor," Nancy said, "or would you rather have us take your husband to the hospital?"

"Oh, no, not yet," the woman replied quickly. "He seems to be coming around."

In a few minutes Mr. Bunce revived. He looked at his audience rather bleary-eyed. Then, as his vision cleared, he frowned deeply.

"How did I get here?" he asked, staring into the faces of his neighbors.

Nancy explained about the girls finding him unconscious in the driveway.

"What happened to you?" she asked.

"I got hit on the head."

"By whom?"

"I don't know," Mr. Bunce answered. "Someone came up behind me. I'm all right now and I've got a headache. I'll thank all of you to go."

"We will," Nancy replied. "But before we leave, will you tell us if you have any idea who hit you?"

"Yes, I have," Bunce answered. "The cat thief. I couldn't sleep, so I decided to go for a walk. I got dressed and went outside. The fellow must have been hiding somewhere around. I heard scuffling in your driveway and thought I'd investigate. The next thing I knew *wham!*"

Mrs. Bealing spoke up. "Mrs. Bunce, are you

sure everything will be all right? One of us will be glad to stay here with you if you think it's necessary."

Fred Bunce answered. "No, no! You all go back to your house. My wife and I will be all right."

Nancy was the last to leave. As she was going out the kitchen door, Mrs. Bunce stopped her and said, "You've asked us so many questions. I have one for you. Why were all of you out in the yard?"

Nancy decided not to give the whole reason. "We couldn't sleep either," she said. "Aren't you glad we found your husband?"

"Oh, yes, of course," Mrs. Bunce said, and closed the door.

When the visitors reached their own house, George remarked, "Neither of the Bunces sounded very grateful for what we did."

"They certainly didn't," Bess agreed. "The two of them acted as if they wanted to get rid of us as soon as possible. Nancy, you're always discovering clues. Did you see anything over there that was suspicious?"

Nancy laughed. "Not a thing."

Hannah Gruen asked Nancy if she thought Bunce had been attacked by the cat thief.

"Possibly. Or even by the tapper. What I can't figure out is why Mr. Bunce was all dressed. It almost seemed as if he planned to go somewhere, but was stopped in his tracks."

George suddenly exclaimed, "We never checked on the cats! We'd better find out if any more have been stolen."

"Oh, I hope not," said Bess.

The girls went outside and unlocked the garage. They counted the cats. All were still there.

"Good," said Bess, relieved. "Miss Carter would really be heartbroken if any more were taken."

The girls finally went back to bed and this time Nancy fell asleep. In the morning she told Miss Carter that the mysterious visitor had tapped out a message to her.

"He dared me to find him. When I asked if he was Gus Woonton, he didn't reply. Not even when I told him I had some valuable information for him."

"Which seems to prove," Miss Carter said, "that the tapper isn't Gus Woonton after all."

Nancy could not agree. She decided to call the Beverly where Gus had been a patient and see if by any chance he had learned Morse code. She phoned and identified herself, then said she might have a clue to Gus Woonton's whereabouts.

Mr. Pratt, the director, said that he did not know if Gus knew Morse code but would find out. He suggested that Nancy call back later that day.

"Tell me," said Nancy, "what your opinion is of Gus Woonton. Would he be bright enough to learn the code and use it?"

"Oh, yes. I'd say Gus is too bright. This is why he is restless and uncontrollable. When he became angry, his emotional instability came out. He would do all sorts of strange things. Well, Miss Drew, I'll wait for your next call." Mr. Pratt said good-by and hung up.

Nancy reported this latest bit of information to Bess and George.

"Then I'll bet," said George, "that Gus Woonton is smart enough to have figured out a secret way to get into this house."

Bess nodded. "Maybe somebody drops him from a helicopter and he comes down the chimney like Santa Claus." The girls grinned.

"It's possible," Nancy remarked, "that the answer lies in the secret room. It took us a long time to find the panel that opened into it. Let's search again and try harder to find an exit. We must check on that beam that I thought moved. Come on!"

The three girls hurried to the basement. First they pushed the ceiling beam sideways, hoping it might move something else that would prove to be an opening. But nothing was revealed.

Next Nancy opened the secret panel. They switched on the lights and let their eyes roam all over the bedroom.

"Maybe the diary has been brought back here," Bess suggested.

Nancy took the key, still on its ribbon around her neck, and unlocked the cupboard. It was empty!

"Oh!" Bess cried out. "That mysterious person took every letter and paper that was here. There was so much he must have had a big sack or a suitcase to put it all in."

"Which means," said George, "that he couldn't get out of a small space. If we find another opening, it would have to be a good-sized one."

Bess remarked, "The person who took the letters and papers must have thought them pretty important to take them away. Nancy, do you think it was because of us?"

"Yes, I do," Nancy answered. "It would have taken us a long time to look through everything. I have an idea that the tapper has been watching us and knew that we hadn't had a chance yet to read every paper."

Bess sighed. "And maybe there was some very valuable information in the papers to help solve this mystery."

Nancy chided herself for not taking time before this to examine the contents of the cupboard. But she decided there was no use dwelling on this now. The girls had come down here to find a possible secret exit.

George, meanwhile, was running a hand along the shelves of the cupboard and the walls back of them. "I thought maybe there might be a spring that would turn this cupboard away from the wall and reveal a way out of here."

She found nothing and now stood on a chair so she could reach way back into the corners.

"This is deep," she said. "Maybe there's a hidden exit—"

The next second the excitement on her face changed to an expression of pain. "Oh!" George cried out.

CHAPTER XIV

Disastrous Rehearsal

NANCY and Bess rushed to George's side. "Are you hurt?" Bess asked her cousin.

"A little," George replied shakily.

With tears welling in her eyes, she pulled her hand from the recesses of the cupboard. On the end of one finger of her right hand hung a strong mousetrap.

"Get it off! Quick! It's killing me!" George begged.

The mousetrap was a new one and had a heavy spring. While Bess held the trap, Nancy pulled up the heavy wire with all her strength. When George pulled back her finger, Nancy let the wire go and the trap flew halfway across the room.

Bess was incensed. "I'll bet Gus Woonton put this here on purpose," she said. "He has an evil mind."

She and Nancy were concerned about George.

"You must put your finger in ice water right away," Nancy told her. "I'll get some ice for you."

"Oh, I can do it," George assured her. "I guess I'm lucky that the trap didn't break my finger."

She insisted upon taking care of the injury herself, so Nancy and Bess continued their hunt for hiding places in the secret bedroom. Nancy swung her flashlight into the area where the mousetrap had been. She could detect nothing but dust in the hidden recess. The rest of the cupboard yielded no clue either.

"Nancy, I guess we'll have to give up," Bess told her chum. "Let's go upstairs and see how George is making out."

"Just a minute," Nancy requested. "Actually we haven't investigated this room and the bath thoroughly."

Every inch of the ceiling, walls, and floor were inspected again. Finally the girls' search was rewarded. They found a loose floor board under the bed. There was a small hollow space beneath it but no treasure lay within.

"If there ever was anything in here," said Nancy, "it has been taken out and I'd guess not long ago."

Finally the girls went upstairs. George was still soaking her finger in the ice water, but Mrs. Bealing had brought a bottle of witch hazel. She soaked a piece of cotton, wound it around George's finger and put on a bandage.

"That should do the trick," she said. "Incidentally, I don't see how any mice could get into that room downstairs. Besides, you say the trap wasn't baited. This means that evil man put it there, hoping to harm somebody."

"And he did," George said ruefully.

Early in the afternoon Nancy telephoned the Beverly. Mr. Pratt told her that Gus Woonton did indeed know Morse code. "He learned it in our craft shop. Please tell me why you inquired about that."

"Because we think that possibly Gus is hiding in this house and may be responsible for the strange tapping-heel sounds we hear at night, sometimes in Morse code. He did spell out one sentence."

"That's a unique situation," Mr. Pratt remarked. "With you and the police and ourselves hunting for Gus, he should be caught soon."

Nancy said she would pass along the latest information about Gus to the authorities, then expressed her thanks and said good-by. Two minutes later she was talking with the sergeant on duty at Berryville Police Headquarters. He said that unfortunately it would not be possible to put a twenty-four-hour stakeout on the Carter home.

"We're short-handed with some of the men on vacation," he explained. "I suggest that Miss Carter engage the services of a private detective agency. Of course we'll take a look around the house every time we go through Amity Place."

Nancy was disappointed. She felt that the police were not taking the mystery seriously enough. Furthermore, she was sure Miss Carter could not afford the services of private detectives.

"We girls will just have to do it ourselves," Nancy decided.

When she mentioned this to Bess and George, the latter said, "But you can't watch tonight, Nancy. You have a rehearsal."

"Yes, I know. But how about you two detectives standing guard?"

The cousins looked at each other. Finally Bess said, "Of course we'll do it, Nancy. George and I will take a nap this evening, then spend the night watching."

When Hannah Gruen heard that Nancy had to return to River Heights that evening and Ned would not be there to take her to the rehearsal, the housekeeper insisted upon going along.

"You've had so many narrow escapes, I want to keep you from any more danger."

Nancy laughed. "You're such a dear, Hannah," she said. "Well, be prepared for anything."

Everyone had an early supper, then Bess and George went to take naps. Mrs. Bealing was to call them at nine o'clock.

Nancy and Hannah left. They were alert to danger all the way, but the ride to River Heights was without incident.

"I'm afraid I cheated you out of some excitement," Nancy told Hannah. "Nobody followed us or tried to harm either of us."

"Thank goodness for that," Hannah said.

They entered the school auditorium. Mrs. Gruen insisted upon sitting in the second row.

Nancy laughed. "The orchestra may make you deaf."

"I'll take that chance," the housekeeper said.

In a few minutes the rehearsal began. The director said it was getting so close to performance time that he had decided to have the scenery set up.

"I want you to get used to it so your movements through doorways and on the stairs will look natural."

As the rehearsal proceeded, Mr. Skank began to nod approvingly at the various performers. Nancy came in for her share of praise for her early tap number.

Her second dance took place near a heavy side wall. It was not raised and lowered by pulleys; but had heavy braces behind it so that it could be pushed to wherever it was needed.

Nancy was about halfway through her number when others on the stage became aware that the wall was teetering. Suddenly it began to fall toward Nancy.

"Look out!" several actors warned.

"Nancy!" Hannah Gruen screamed.

Instinctively Nancy glanced over her shoulder. She was horrified at what she saw. It was not possible to escape the falling wall!

Instantly four quick-witted young men sprang forward. Two caught the front end of the wall, the others the rear. Carefully they eased it to the floor.

Mr. Skank rushed over. "Are you all right?" he asked Nancy.

She nodded, then said, "I wonder what caused the set to fall."

"Somebody's carelessness," the director replied angrily. "I'm going to find out!"

One of the young actresses, who had been backstage, came running forward. She said that a short, heavy-set man who was not connected with the play had been leaning against the wall.

"The next thing I knew the scenery was falling. It almost seemed as if he had done it on purpose."

"Where is he now?" the director asked.

The girl said he had run away as soon as the wall had started to tumble.

Everyone rushed from the stage to find the man, but he had disappeared. Nancy said nothing to the others but she had a strong hunch he might have been Gus Woonton and that he had intended to harm her.

"He's really dangerous," she told herself. An involuntary shiver went down her spine as she thought of perhaps meeting him face to face.

Suddenly the wall began to fall toward Nancy!

The wall was put back in place and the rehearsal continued. By the time it was over, Nancy had begun to feel hungry. It had been hours since the early supper at Miss Carter's house.

As she and Hannah started off in the car, Nancy said, "Let's stop at Finch's Soda Shop for ice-cream sundaes."

Mrs. Gruen laughed. "I'm kind of hungry myself," she admitted. "But Finch's is a place for young people."

Nancy patted Hannah's hand. "There's always room for you with this young person." Mrs. Gruen beamed.

When they walked in, all the tables were taken, so the two seated themselves on stools at the counter.

"Hi, Roscoe!" Nancy said to the clerk. "Two vanillas with fudge sauce, please. We're starved. How about some of your good cookies, too?"

"Coming right up," Roscoe replied. Then he leaned across the counter and whispered to Nancy, "The police were here looking for you. They missed you at the school and thought you might stop here."

"Did the officers say what they wanted?" Nancy asked.

"Yes. The sergeant is expecting you at headquarters to identify a burglar."

CHAPTER XV

The New Lead

ROSCOE had the sundaes ready in a jiffy. "Eat up," he said. "You'll need your strength to face that burglar!" A broad grin spread over the clerk's face.

Nancy smiled back. "I'd say I have the advantage because he's behind bars."

"You win," said Roscoe. "I might have known better than to try getting ahead of you. Working on a new mystery?"

"Yes. Got any clues?"

"What kind?" the clerk asked, his eyes twinkling. "I have all sorts of clues filed away."

The subject was not pursued, because new customers came in and Roscoe had to wait on them.

"We'd better hurry," Nancy told Hannah. "I wonder if the suspect the police are holding is Gus Woonton."

She and Mrs. Gruen ate quickly. Nancy paid the clerk and they left the soda shop.

When they reached headquarters, a sergeant, named Scott, whom Nancy had never seen before, was on duty. She introduced herself and Mrs. Gruen, and the officer said he would call a man to take them to the cell block.

"A pudgy man was brought in a short time ago," he explained. "He hasn't gone to bed yet. Tell me if you recognize him or have ever seen him around here or in Berryville."

The two visitors were led along the cell block. Most of the prisoners were asleep. The guard stopped in front of the cell in which the suspect sat. His light was still on.

Nancy got only a quick glimpse of his face because he instantly turned his back. The guard ordered the prisoner to come forward but he refused. The officer tried to make him talk, but got no response.

"Never mind," Nancy whispered to the guard. "I'm sure I haven't seen this man before, either here or in Berryville. How about you, Hannah?"

The Drews' housekeeper shook her head. She and Nancy were ushered back to the main room and told Sergeant Scott that they could not identify the suspect.

"What name did he give you?" Nancy asked.

"He refused to give any," the sergeant replied.

"He was picked up tonight trying to rob a jewelry store. Chief McGinnis told us you're looking for a pudgy suspect, so I thought this man might be the one."

"I don't believe so," Nancy said, "but you might try a trick on him. The one we're looking for knows Morse code. If you could have someone casually tap out words on a telegrapher's key and make a mistake while the prisoner is listening, he might involuntarily speak up and give himself away."

"Thanks for the tip," the sergeant said. "We'll try it. If we have any luck, I'll let you know."

Nancy and Mrs. Gruen went home. Mr. Drew was still up, waiting to tell them what he had learned that day about the case. First, the lawyer listened eagerly to his daughter's story, then said he had some news of his own for her.

"Toby Simpson was a great help to me and came up with some good leads. He learned that Mr. and Mrs. Woonton, although they had lived in St. Louis, had passed away in Chicago.

"After calling two of my lawyer friends there," Mr. Drew went on, "I found out that an administrator had been appointed for their son Gus. And guess what the administrator's name is?"

"I can't imagine," Nancy replied. "Who is it? Man or woman?"

"A man named W. F. Bunce."

Nancy was startled and leaned forward eagerly. "You mean he might be the Mr. Bunce who lives next door to Miss Carter?"

"He could be," the lawyer answered, "but let's not jump to conclusions. At the time he was appointed administrator W. F. Bunce lived in St. Louis.

"After I'd made several more phone calls, it seemed evident that he had moved away from there sometime ago. No W. F. Bunce was listed in the St. Louis telephone directory nor did he have an unlisted number. And the post office had no forwarding address."

"How did you find out he had been appointed administrator?" Nancy queried.

"William Woonton's will was probated in Chicago. W. F. Bunce was left in total charge of the estate. He was both executor and administrator. You know I don't like to be suspicious, but when I learned that payments to the Beverly stopped at the time of the Woontons' deaths—they were killed in an automobile accident—I began to wonder about this W. F. Bunce."

Nancy was excited by the latest clue and eager to pursue it. Her father said he must be at his office early the next morning and would leave the follow-up to her. First she looked in the phone book covering Berryville. No W. F. Bunce was listed; only Frederick Bunce.

The idea of a ruse to trap him popped into Nancy's mind. She said to Mrs. Gruen, "Will you do me a big favor, Hannah?" Nancy glanced at her wrist watch. "It's only eleven o'clock. Will you please telephone Fred Bunce's house and ask if it is the residence of W. F. Bunce."

"Suppose the person who answers says yes," Hannah remarked. "Then what do I do?"

"Say that someone will bring an important message to Mr. Bunce tomorrow morning."

Mrs. Gruen was a bit nervous about making the call, but she dialed the number and waited.

Mrs. Bunce answered the phone. "Hello?"

Hannah Gruen spoke in as deep a voice as she could and asked, "Is this the residence of W. F. Bunce?"

There was a startled cry from the other end of the wire, then Mrs. Bunce said, "Uh—no. You have the wrong number." She hung up.

"Ah-ha!" said the housekeeper. "Nancy, I think you've hit upon something important. Do you suppose Fred Bunce really is the W. F. Bunce you're looking for?"

Nancy thought this quite possible. The question was, Why had he moved next door to the Woontons' former residence? Could he be the person who was entering mysteriously and hunting for some hidden treasures?

The housekeeper sighed. "This thing is getting

so mixed up I can't make head nor tail of who's who or what's what. When is it ever going to be straightened out?"

"I feel the same way," Nancy agreed. "I can't wait to follow up this new lead."

Before Nancy started off for Miss Carter's the next day, Mrs. Gruen said, "Do be careful. Put up the top of your convertible and lock yourself in."

"All right and don't worry. I hope the next time I talk to you, I can report that the mystery's solved."

Nancy packed a few extra clothes, then kissed Hannah good-by and drove to Berryville. Bess and George were waiting in the driveway when she reached Miss Carter's house.

"Hi, girls!" Nancy called out. "I'm surprised that you're still up. You should be getting some sleep. Tell me, did anything happen last night?"

"Not a thing," Bess replied. "No cat thief, no tapper, nobody sneaking around."

"The only thing interesting," George put in, "were the lights in the Bunces's house."

"What do you mean?"

George said she doubted that the Bunces went to bed at all. "Lights were popping on and off in various rooms most of the night. I wonder what they were doing."

Nancy told about her latest lead in the mystery which concerned a W. F. Bunce, whom she suspected might be Fred Bunce. The other girls were amazed.

"What are you going to do about it?" Bess asked her.

"You say the couple was up during the night?" Nancy replied with a faraway look. "Well, maybe they're asleep now. All the shades on this side of the house are drawn."

George told her that the shades had been drawn throughout the house. "A couple of times I went out of the garage and walked around for exercise. I noticed that every shade in the place was down."

Nancy wondered how long to wait before going next door to learn what she could about the couple. It was now nine forty-five.

"I think ten o'clock is late enough," she decided.

Fifteen minutes later the girls knocked on the rear door. There was no response. They tried the front doorbell. The Bunces did not answer this, either.

Nancy used the door knocker. It resounded loudly. Still no one appeared.

"Do you suppose they're still asleep with all this racket?" Bess asked.

Nancy shrugged. "George, would you go back to Miss Carter's and phone the Bunces? That should wake them up."

George hurried inside but returned in a few minutes, saying there had been no response.

"Maybe the couple has gone out," Nancy said. "I'll look in their garage."

The doors were closed but she peered through a window. There was no car inside.

It occurred to Nancy that possibly Hannah Gruen's telephone call to the Bunces the night before had frightened them and they had left. At that moment a neighbor on the other side of the house came out.

"Are you looking for Mr. and Mrs. Bunce?" she asked.

"Yes," Nancy replied. "We're staying with Miss Carter and wanted to speak to them."

"Well, I'm afraid that's impossible," the neighbor said. "About six o'clock this morning a truck came here. The driver loaded it with a lot of boxes and bags. The Bunces followed in their car."

"By any chance do you know the license number of the Bunces's car?" Nancy asked the woman.

"Funny you should ask that and I can say yes. I remember it because the letters in it happen to be my initials and the numbers are the reverse of those on my car." She gave the full license number.

"Thank you very much," Nancy said. "And now please excuse me. I must hurry inside and make a phone call."

She dashed into the house and dialed her

father. "Oh, Dad, we've missed again!" she said woefully. "But here's the Bunces's license number. Perhaps you can check to whom it was issued and maybe the police can stop the car before it disappears."

Mr. Drew said he would check the name of the owner. As for stopping the couple on the road, he had no right to ask this.

"We have no concrete evidence against Mr. Bunce, nothing but suspicions," he reminded his daughter. "But I'll let you know what I find out."

When Nancy finished talking, Bess asked, "Do you mind if I use your car? I have some errands to do downtown. Marketing—and I must buy more cat food for the pets."

"Go ahead," Nancy replied.

Nancy went upstairs to say good morning to Miss Carter and brief her on the latest event. The actress was astonished at the news.

"Well, if Bunce was the tapper," she said, "then we won't hear him again. Maybe it's just as well that he's gone. He hated my cats, anyway."

A few minutes later George joined them and the two girls went to dust their rooms. Nancy stopped to talk to her friend while George made her bed.

"Listen!" she said suddenly.

This time the strange sound was not tapping. It was more like a weird plaintive wail.

Both girls stood still. Nancy pointed upward and whispered, "Something or somebody is in the attic!"

The girls tiptoed to the door of the third-floor stairway. It was open a few inches. They paused a moment, then started up the steps. Wondering what they would find, the girls stood at the top of the stairs and stared ahead.

The queer sounds were coming from inside the wooden mummy case, which was wobbling back and forth!

CHAPTER XVI

Telltale Handprints

WITH cautious steps Nancy and George approached the wobbling mummy case. It was locked on the outside.

The wailing within had now intensified. Had a person been imprisoned? Yet the sounds did not seem human.

Taking a long breath, Nancy opened the latch on the mummy case. A wild-eyed Persian cat leaped out!

"Oh!" the girls exclaimed.

Then Nancy and George began to laugh. George said, "Boy, I'm something! I can't tell the difference between a cat and a ghost!"

Apparently the cat had been imprisoned for some time and refused to quiet down. Even though Nancy held out a friendly hand, the Persian would not come near her.

"How in the world did it get up here?" George

asked. "Somebody must have deliberately locked it in the mummy case. But who?"

"It's a good thing that case isn't airtight," Nancy said.

"Do you suppose," George asked, "the tapper put the cat in there for spite?"

Nancy shook her head. "I'm sure he has nothing against Miss Carter or the cat. Possibly he has stolen some, but I think his main objective in coming here is to find valuable objects hidden in this house."

George wondered if Mr. and Mrs. Woonton, having such an unpredictable son, had secreted some of their valuables. "Gus may have figured his parents forgot to take them along when they moved, and he is now trying to locate the pieces and perhaps sell them. Or does he know his parents are dead and he has come to get the articles?"

"It's a good hunch," Nancy replied. "Here's another idea. Remember the threat in Gus's diary of getting square with his guardians? Maybe he managed to get out of the secret room at times and hid the articles to make the guardians seem like thieves. And now he's back to collect them."

All this time she had been coaxing the cat to come toward her. Finally it walked to where she was standing. Nancy picked up the Persian and the two girls went back to the second floor. When Miss Carter heard the story, she gasped.

"Every day this mystery becomes more of a

puzzle," she said. "You girls are doing a good job, but I wish that the unwanted stranger would stop coming into the house." She took the cat on her lap. "You poor tabby," she said. "You might have been smothered. Oh, there are such wicked people in this world!"

Just then Mrs. Bealing appeared in the doorway. She had heard only part of the conversation and wanted to know what had happened. When Nancy explained, a look of dismay spread over the nurse's face.

"I'm afraid that I locked the cat inside the mummy case," she said. "I went upstairs to get some rags. The case was open so I locked it." She gave a great sigh. "Oh, I never would have forgiven myself if this beautiful animal had died because of me."

Miss Carter spoke up quickly. "How were you to know? What I want to find out is who brought the cat into the house."

No one had an answer. While they were still discussing the incident, Bess came into the driveway. She deposited her packages on the kitchen counter and went upstairs.

When she reached the second floor, Mrs. Bealing burst out with the story of the cat in the mummy case. "I'd certainly like to know who brought that Persian into the house!"

Bess was aghast and hung her head. "I did," she said. "The poor thing didn't seem very well, so I took it to my room. You were asleep, so I decided to tell you later. I guess the cat went up to the third floor by itself."

Miss Carter was relieved. "Such a simple explanation for what started out to be a big mystery," she remarked.

Bess said, "I stopped at the pet shop downtown and asked the man what to do for a sick cat. He gave me this special food." She held up the package.

By now the cat had gone into a deep sleep on Miss Carter's lap. For a moment everyone wondered if perhaps the Persian had been drugged like the others. But when the actress roused the cat, it stretched, yawned, then jumped from her lap.

"It seems to be all right," she remarked. "But go ahead and give my pet some of the special food you bought, Bess."

As Miss Carter watched the Persian daintily eating the tidbits, she said that the mummy case had been used in the play *The Dancer and the Fool.*

"I wonder if Toby Simpson might like to use it in his revival of the play. I think I'll phone him later today."

Just then the phone rang. Mr. Drew was calling Nancy. "I have some further information for you," he said. "It's rather startling."

"What is it?" Nancy asked quickly.

The lawyer said that something he had learned only complicated the case. "The license for the Bunces's car was issued in Pleasantville to a Gus Woonton."

"What!" Nancy exclaimed. "Dad, do you think that the Bunces and Gus Woonton are together?"

"Either that, or Bunce is using Woonton's name."

"I'd say," Nancy put in, "that whichever is true, it proves that the Fred Bunce we know is the administrator of the Woonton estate."

The lawyer said he had checked the Pleasantville address given to him by the license bureau but that neither Gus Woonton nor anyone named Bunce was known there.

"So it's apparent Bunce or Gus Woonton gave a phony address."

Mr. Drew also said that he planned to ask the St. Louis and Chicago authorities for further information on William Woonton's will.

"I'll start right away," he promised. "Take care. Good-by."

Nancy sat lost in thought for some time. There were many clues and many leads in this puzzling mystery, but at the moment they seemed to have led only to dead ends. She finally roused herself and went to report the latest findings to her friends.

Bess sensed at once that the girl detective was discouraged. "Nancy," she said, "a change from thinking about all this would do you good." She turned to Miss Carter. "Would you mind if we girls go to the attic and look over the rest of the props?"

The actress smiled. "I think that would be a splendid idea. But I want to go with you. I'd like to explain what some of the things are and in what plays they were used."

Nancy and George carried the frail woman to the third floor. There was an old, worn couch and she asked to be placed on it.

"This stood in the living room of a scene in the stage production of *Three Votes for Mary*. In that play I was trying to get a friend of mine elected. And oh the exaggerations I told about her!" The actress laughed gaily at the recollection.

She pointed to a large trunk. "That's full of costumes," she said.

"Oh, may I try on some of them?" Bess asked.

Miss Carter smiled and said, "No offense, dear, but all of them were worn by me. You will admit that our—our figures aren't exactly the same."

Bess admitted this but opened the trunk and took out the gowns one by one. There was such a variety that she remarked, "Miss Carter, you were a queen, a dairy maid, a soldier—"

"Yes, I even played the part of a boy soldier. I wasn't supposed to be in the play. The agency called me in a hurry because the actor became ill."

"How did you manage to talk like a young man?" George asked.

"I didn't. I merely moved my lips and a young man offstage said the lines."

Although Bess could not wear any of the gowns, she held them up in front of her and looked in a full-length mirror at herself.

"I'm Queen Elizabeth," she said. After putting the gorgeous white satin dress back in the trunk, she picked up a robe such as judges wear. "Who am I now?"

"Portia in *The Merchant of Venice* by Shakespeare," Miss Carter replied.

Nancy had been listening, but all the time her eyes kept roaming around hunting for clues. Without disturbing the others, she began to move boxes and trunks quietly. There was no sign of a trap door in the floor.

As Nancy moved a chest aside which stood in front of a window, her attention was drawn to the sill. Although the window was closed, there were clear signs of hand- and footprints, indicating that someone had entered the attic this way. She opened the window which had no lock on it, and found more prints on the outside sill.

"Girls, come here!" she called out. "I think I've found something important!"

Bess and George rushed over and stared at the marks. Then Bess exclaimed, "If anybody climbed up here from the ground, he must be a monkey!"

"Who can open windows," George added. "Of course we have no idea how long these prints have been here. Someone could have climbed up a ladder before we came on the case."

"That's true," Nancy conceded, "but I have a hunch these marks were made recently." Her eyes lighted up. "I'm going to rig something to try catching anybody who comes in this way again."

Nancy explained her scheme. She would attach an unseen cord to the window and run it down to her bedroom.

"If anybody opens this window," she said, "it will ring a bell near me. Then I can race up here and grab him."

"Not without me," George spoke up firmly.

"All right," Nancy agreed.

Later, as the girls prepared for bed, they wondered if there would be a visitor that night. They fell asleep. Around one o'clock in the morning Nancy's bell began to ring!

CHAPTER XVII

Rooftop Escape

IN a jiffy Nancy was out of bed and putting on robe and slippers. She dashed into the room where Bess and George were sleeping and woke them.

"What's up?" George asked.

"The bell rang!" Nancy whispered. "Come on! Hurry!"

She was more than halfway up the attic steps before the girls overtook her. Nancy beamed her flashlight into every dark corner of the attic, since the overhead light was a dim one. No one was hiding there.

"Maybe when the tapper heard the bell," Bess suggested, "it scared him and he went back out the window. Let's see if he's hanging on."

They rushed over and looked out. There was no sign of an intruder.

"Of course he had plenty of time to get down," George remarked.

Nancy reminded the others it was a pretty precarious climb hanging onto a vertical wall. "It couldn't be done quickly."

"Right," said Bess. "And I don't see how he could do it, anyway."

Puzzled, the girls gazed across the roof. They could see only part of it, since the house had two gables. The moon was shining and everything stood out clearly.

Suddenly George grabbed Nancy's arm. "Look! Over by the chimney! There he goes!"

For a few seconds a pudgy figure was silhouetted on a far peak. Then it disappeared.

"We can catch him yet!" Nancy exclaimed. "He can't get down as fast as we can."

She led the way downstairs, two steps at a time. The girls dashed to the first floor and outside.

Taking opposite directions they raced around the house, all the time looking upward for the climbing figure. In the bright moonlight they could not have missed anyone descending from the roof, yet no person was visible.

"He's gone again!" Bess wailed. "I don't fancy running into somebody dangerous, but just the same I'd like to know who the climber is and how he gets up and down."

At that moment they heard a motor start and hurried to the street. A car, which was not the Bunces's, pulled away from in front of their house with a roar.

The driver, who had no passenger, held a hand over the side of his face so he could not be identified. He suddenly turned out his lights, making it impossible for the girls to read his license number.

"Now who was he?" George asked. "Perhaps Fred Bunce came back for more of his things."

"I doubt it," Bess replied. "He must know by now that the police are looking for him. He wouldn't dare come here."

"It might have been the pudgy man we saw on the roof," Nancy remarked.

"What do we do now?" Bess asked.

Nancy said she was going to alert the police. Two officers arrived in a little while and Nancy briefed them on the details of the man who had been on the roof and escaped. The police made a thorough search of the entire house, even the secret room, which Nancy showed them.

"Man alive! What a prison!" one of the officers exclaimed. "Staying in here for any length of time is enough to drive a person crazy even if he didn't start that way."

Nancy made no comment. At times she felt sorry for Gus Woonton and figured that if he had had psychiatric help as a child he might not have turned out the way he had.

"It may not be too late," she thought but kept the supposition to herself.

Finally the two officers, convinced that the intruder had gone, said they must leave but would check the house again in about an hour.

"If you hear anybody in the meantime, let us know," one said.

The commotion had awakened Miss Carter and Mrs. Bealing, who wanted to know what had happened. They were given a full report.

At the end Nancy said, "Unfortunately we've learned almost nothing. But the tapper—or whoever got into the attic—knows by now we've rigged up a way to snare him. So I figure there's a good chance he won't be back."

Actually Nancy said this to allay the women's fears but deep in her heart she did not believe it. Anyone as determined as the tapper would return.

Finally everyone went to bed for the second time that night. There was absolute silence in the house. Nancy did not drop off to sleep at once. Suddenly she jumped from the bed and started for the hall doorway.

She had heard tapping-heel sounds on the second floor!

By the time Nancy reached the hall, the tapping had stopped. She waited. There was not a sound.

An eerie feeling came over Nancy, as if she were being watched by unseen eyes. The young sleuth stood still for a long time, but there was not another sound either from the second floor or anywhere else in the house.

"I couldn't have dreamed hearing the tapping," she thought, going back to her room and dropping into bed.

Nancy did not get much rest that night. The mystery had begun to disturb her. She felt she was getting nowhere in solving it. Finally, utterly weary, Nancy fell asleep.

She had promised to take Mrs. Bealing to River Heights early in the morning so the woman could spend Sunday at home. Nancy was up, bathed, and dressed before anyone else was ready.

Bess and George had promised to care for Miss Carter while her nurse was gone. They planned to hurry with the housework because in the afternoon their Emerson college friends, Burt Eddleton and Dave Evans, would arrive and stay to supper. Ned had told Nancy he would come to her house by bus and the two would drive to Berryville in her car.

"I'll ride back to Emerson with the boys," he had said.

Before Nancy and Mrs. Bealing left, Miss Carter again thanked them for all they had done.

"I'll try not to be any trouble to Bess and George," she said. "If they get too lonesome, I'll try to cheer them up by quoting a few humorous lines from plays I've been in."

"That'll be great," Bess replied with a giggle.

She felt unusually happy this morning. It was a clear day and birds were singing cheerily. She had succeeded in playing Cupid for Toby Simpson and Miss Carter. And in a few hours her favorite date would arrive.

"You look," George said to her cousin, "like a satisfied cat who has just finished off a poor mouse."

"Yes? Well, how about you doing a little grinning?" Bess retorted. "Burt'll like that."

Nancy and Mrs. Bealing said good-by and left the house. As they rode along, Mrs. Bealing said, "This is a beautiful morning, isn't it? We're having special services at our church. I'm so glad Miss Carter gave me the day off."

Suddenly she asked Nancy, "Do you always go to church?"

"As often as I can," she replied. "This morning Dad and Hannah and I will go to service together."

"That's nice."

When Nancy reached home, Mrs. Gruen insisted that she have a second breakfast—at least some of her homemade coffee cake.

Nancy laughed. "I can't very well refuse that, although I did eat a big breakfast."

After church Nancy helped with dinner preparations and by one o'clock she and her father and Mrs. Gruen were sitting down to a delicious meal of roast lamb, mashed potatoes, fresh peas, and strawberry shortcake.

"Marvelous dinner," Mr. Drew said.

Directly afterward Nancy put the plates, glasses, and silver into the dishwasher. Meanwhile the housekeeper had begun preparations for a cold supper which Nancy would take with her. By this time Mrs. Gruen knew the favorite foods of the three boys who were coming to Miss Carter's.

"This evening there'll be chicken sandwiches, sliced tomatoes, and apple pie with ice cream," she announced.

"Perfect," said Nancy.

An hour later the telephone rang. Mr. Drew answered. He talked a long while and then came out to the kitchen.

"That call was from St. Louis," he said. "Here's big news. As soon as the Woonton estate was settled—and there were no complications—W. F. Bunce, the money and the stocks and bonds vanished."

"Oh dear!" Nancy exclaimed. "Does this mean he stole them?"

The lawyer shrugged. "It certainly makes everything harder to figure out."

Nancy knit her brow. "If Bunce stole them, why did he take a chance on getting caught by ignoring the Beverly? It seems to me it would have been smarter if he had paid Gus Woonton's board. Then no one would have become suspicious."

"You're absolutely right, Nancy," her father agreed. "And this also doesn't explain why, if

Miss Carter's neighbor is W. F. Bunce, he came to live in Berryville where the old Woonton house is. According to the reports, there was a lot of money in the estate and I should have thought he would have gone as far away as possible."

The discussion was interrupted by loud banging on the kitchen door. Nancy opened it. Her young friend Tommy Johnson was standing there. His eyes were large and he was so excited he could hardly talk. He stuttered and stammered something unintelligible.

"What is it, Tommy?" Nancy asked. "Say it slowly."

The little boy pointed toward the garage. "I just saw a man sneak out of there, and now I can hear something ticking!"

CHAPTER XVIII

Spikes of a Human Fly

As the Drews raced toward the garage, Nancy's father cried out, "It could be a bomb! You'd better stay here!"

"Oh, Dad, please!" she begged. "You mustn't run into danger either."

The two reached the garage at the same moment. The ticking was loud. It was definitely coming from beneath Nancy's car. Mr. Drew grabbed a rake and began to pull the ticking object from beneath the automobile.

"It isn't worth risking your life, Dad," Nancy cried out.

With a deft sweep of his arms, her father swung the bomb onto the lawn. It rolled away.

"The ticking is dying down," he said. "I'm sure the bomb's not going to explode. In rolling it over, I probably partly deactivated it."

A few seconds later the ticking stopped entirely. Mr. Drew walked over and began taking the object apart.

"Why, Dad—" Nancy began, alarmed.

The lawyer laughed. "A few years ago I took some instructions in deactivating bombs," he explained. "I thought it might come in handy some time, but I admit I never thought it would be right in my own garage."

Mr. Drew confirmed his guess that by rolling the bomb he had moved a switch on the inside. It had slowed the ticking.

"Dad, if you hadn't disarmed the bomb, when would it have gone off?"

"I can't be sure, of course," her father replied, "but from this timer in her I'd say in about ten minutes."

Suddenly Nancy remembered Tommy who had given them the warning. Where was he? Just then he came out the back door with Mrs. Gruen.

The little boy began to complain about Hannah. "She wouldn't let me come out and see the fun," he said.

"And she did the right thing," Mr. Drew spoke up. "Tommy, it's a good thing you noticed the ticking sound or Nancy's car would have been blown to smithereens."

"What!" Tommy cried out. "Was it a bomb I heard?"

"It sure was," Nancy replied. "Tommy, you

said you saw a man sneaking away from the garage. What did he look like?"

Tommy could not give a very detailed description of him, but it tallied closely with that of Fred Bunce. If it was he, what had he hoped to gain by blowing up her car?

Upon reflection Nancy told herself, "It would be a little hard for me to get around without a car. But then I could have rented one. I believe Fred Bunce had some other reason for coming here."

She could think of none and turned to Tommy. Putting her arms around him, she said, "You're a brave little detective, Tommy. Keep it up and maybe someday you and I can solve a big case together."

"Really? You mean it?" the little boy asked. "That would be groovy."

While Mr. Drew was still working to dismantle the bomb completely, he asked Nancy to get in touch with the police and request that an officer drop over as soon as possible.

"Anyone who plants a bomb should be listed on the police blotter and a hunt for him started," the lawyer said.

Nancy had just finished making the phone call when Ned Nickerson arrived. She said lightly, "We almost didn't have a car to ride in."

"What do you mean?"

Nancy briefed him on the recent happening.

Ned was worried. "You don't seem to be safe anywhere."

Nancy smiled. "Now, Ned, I always get out of these scrapes, don't I?" Then she changed the subject. "We'd better start for Berryville. Ned, will you help carry out our supper?"

When he saw the boxes of sandwiches and pie and the container of ice cream he laughed. "That's enough food to feed an army."

Hannah Gruen spoke up. "I know you boys. I'll bet there won't be a crumb left of what's packed in here."

"We'll sure do our best to make your prediction come true," Ned told her with a laugh.

When he and Nancy reached Miss Carter's house, they found Bess, George, and their dates walking out to feed the cats. They all stopped to look through the huge wire cage.

"Aren't the Persians marvelous?" Bess asked.

"I guess so," Dave replied without enthusiasm. He was a rangy athlete. "But give me a nice big dog for a pal."

Ned and Burt showed only mild interest in the pets. But when the girls took the three boys on a walk around the outside of the house and explained the mysterious happenings, they became intrigued.

"You say one of the men who came here wore spiked shoes?" Ned asked.

"Yes," Nancy replied, "but we don't know

which one he was. There are now at least three suspects."

All the boys were interested in this particular fact. Burt remarked, "It's obvious the fellow had some special reason for wearing spiked shoes and it wasn't for stealing cats."

Suddenly an idea came to Nancy. She began to examine the wall of the house under the window where she had found the hand- and footprints.

"Look here!" she called.

The others rushed over. Nancy pointed out deep gouges in the brickwork.

"Do you suppose the person who wore those shoes used them as spikes to climb up here?"

"He could have," Ned conceded. "But I still don't see how he could have kept his balance."

Dave had been examining the wall. Now he began to take measurements between the gouges. "Do you know what I think?" he asked.

"What?" the others asked.

"That the climber had something over his hands that he could use to dig into the brickwork, as well as the spikes on his shoes."

The six young people examined the wall closely and agreed.

Burt shook his head. "Just the same, I wouldn't want to try climbing up this wall with spikes or claws or anything else. Give me a real safe elevator."

His friends laughed. Bess, proud of her date's

discovery, tucked her arm into his and led him into the house.

She and George had set the table earlier. Ned carried Miss Carter downstairs and then a merry supper party began.

For a time the mysteries were put aside and only wisecracks and teasing remarks flew back and forth. Miss Carter was immensely amused and laughed heartily. The group had just finished eating their apple pie topped with ice cream when the front doorbell rang.

Everyone looked questioningly at the others, except the actress. With a happy smile, she said, "I'm expecting Toby Simpson. He wants to inspect the mummy case and see if it can be used in the revival of *The Dancer and the Fool.*"

The actor was introduced to the boys and talk resumed while the girls cleared the table. The Emerson trio found Mr. Simpson very entertaining.

When the girls returned, the actor said he was ready to look at the mummy case in the attic. Miss Carter insisted upon going along and asked Nancy and Ned to accompany the couple. Once more the actress was placed on the old couch.

Nancy chuckled. "The last occupant of that mummy case was alive," she said. At Toby Simpson's questioning look, she said, "One of Miss Carter's cats got locked in there by mistake."

The actor laughed. Then, after examining the

Engraved on the chest was the name Woonton!

case, he declared it to be in very good condition and said, "Indeed I can use it in the revival. It's pretty valuable so I'll leave it here until we're ready to go into rehearsal."

He looked around at all the other props, saying he was amazed at their good condition. He stopped in front of a large chest.

"Was this used in one of your plays?" he asked Miss Carter.

"No. But if you're interested in borrowing it, help yourself."

The actor said he would like to use the chest in the revival, and would take it along with him right now.

"I'll empty it for you," he said, raising the lid.

Nancy was standing next to him. As he opened the chest wide, she gasped. On top of several boxes stood a smaller chest with a silver nameplate.

Engraved on it was the name Woonton!

"Is something wrong?" Miss Carter called.

Nancy explained what they had found inside the big chest and asked if the actress knew anything about it.

"Why, no. I have never locked that chest and haven't looked in it since I moved here. Someone must have put the little chest inside."

The group speculated on who had put the Woonton chest inside and when.

"It's my guess," said Nancy, "that Gus found this chest hidden somewhere in the house and planned to take it along. He was interrupted or couldn't carry it at the time and quickly hid the chest in here."

Ned spoke up. "If it's unlocked, don't you think we should find out what's inside?"

"Indeed I do," the actress answered. "Bring the little chest here please, so I can see what is in it."

Ned carried it over. The chest proved to be fairly heavy. Miss Carter lifted the lid and everyone exclaimed in surprise at the contents. There was a quantity of beautiful jewelry and several carefully wrapped, priceless figurines.

"Maybe we should turn these over to the police," Miss Carter suggested.

Nancy requested that she not do so immediately. "I'm sure that somebody will be back here to get them. Why don't we return them to your big chest and then set up a twenty-four-hour watch?"

CHAPTER XIX

An Unexpected Solution

EVERYONE was eager to help Nancy trap whoever might come for the Woonton jewels. But Toby Simpson said he would have to be excused. He had been up late the night before and must rise early Monday morning for a rehearsal.

"It's rather a long drive to my place so I must go," the actor told them. "But I wish all of you luck this time in capturing the thief. I'll ask Violette to phone me the outcome."

After he had left, the couples talked over the vantage points where they would station themselves. George was so sure the secret room had something to do with the entry of the tapper that she requested a post there.

"All right," Nancy agreed. Then she said to Burt with a grin, "You'd better go with her and be sure nobody hits her over the head!"

Since every door and window on the first floor was locked, Bess and Dave chose to stand watch on the second floor.

"I wish we had enough people to patrol the outside of the house too," Dave remarked.

Nancy told him she was depending on the police to do this. Then she added, "Ned, how about you and I guarding the attic?"

"Sure thing. Personally I'm sure that's where our thief will be entering."

Miss Carter reluctantly went to bed. "I'm sorry I'm unable to act as a guard," she said.

The lights in the house were put out and the young people went to their various posts. All had agreed not to have any conversation—it might give away the plan of capture.

Nancy and Ned had taken positions on opposite sides of the attic. Ned sat down on the floor near the window where the hand- and footprints had been found. Anyone entering by this means would be surprised with a hard football tackle. Secretly Ned hoped he would have the chance.

Nancy stood near a chimney, From there she could watch the stairway and two other windows. Becoming weary, she sat down and leaned against the brickwork As time dragged by, she found it more and more difficult to keep from falling asleep.

"I'd better stand up for a while," she said to herself. "It'll be easier to stay awake that way."

A few minutes later she wondered if her imagination was playing tricks on her. She had felt a movement on the floor beneath her feet.

"Am I standing on a trap door we didn't discover?" she asked herself, and moved aside with utmost caution.

To her astonishment a section of the floor next to the chimney rose slowly. There was a very faint squeaking sound which attracted Ned's attention at once.

In a moment the couple saw a pudgy man, flashlight in hand, emerge from a stairway! Nancy and Ned hoped that the light would not reveal them. They wanted to wait and see what the intruder would do before tackling him.

"He must be Gus Woonton!" Nancy thought, hardly daring to breathe. "I'll bet he's after the jewels. And when he tries to take them away, we'll pounce on him."

The suspect moved forward. He opened the chest and picked up the smaller box.

Nancy decided it was time for her and Ned to act. In the now dimly lighted attic she waved at Ned, and within two seconds he had the pudgy man on the floor. The victim lost his flashlight and struggled furiously, but Ned held him down.

"Let me up! Let me go! You've got no right here. What do you think you're doing?" the infuriated prisoner cried out. "This chest belongs to me!"

Nancy had walked toward him. She picked up the flashlight and beamed it directly at the man.

"You're Gus Woonton, aren't you? And you came for this little chest of jewels."

"So what if I am and so what if I did?" the man answered. "Those jewels rightfully belong to me. My grandmother gave me the whole chest but my parents wouldn't let me have it. Or anything else she left me, either. Then they went away and left me with guardians, who were cruel. But I got square with them!"

"That's what you wrote in your diary," Nancy remarked. "If you'll promise not to fight any more and go downstairs quietly with us, we'd like to hear your story."

"All right," Gus said solemnly. He gave a hollow laugh. "I thought one place nobody would ever find was the secret stairway I came up."

"Where does it lead?" Ned asked.

Gus explained that originally it had opened into the kitchen but the entrance had been sealed off years ago.

"I hid food in there," Gus explained. "Whenever you went searching in the attic, I'd hide on the steps. One time you almost caught me, so I stepped out on the roof and stayed there until you went downstairs. Then I came back in and you never saw me."

"But three of us did last night," Nancy said.

"Tell me, how did you get into the house with all the doors and windows locked?"

Gus smirked. "You're so good at figuring things out, why don't you try and guess how?"

"That's an easy one," Nancy answered. "You wore spiked golf shoes and fastened spikes to your hands and climbed up the brick wall, then came through that window over there."

Gus was so amazed he stared in stupefaction at Nancy. "Girls aren't supposed to be so bright," he said sullenly.

Nancy could not keep from laughing and Ned remarked, "Gus, I think you'll have to change your mind on that one."

"Did you ever steal any cats?" Nancy questioned.

"No. But I went to the cage once and looked at them."

"When you had on your spiked shoes?"

"Yes."

So the cat thief had not worn golf shoes, Nancy decided.

She asked Gus, "What did you do with all the papers in your secret room?"

"Took them to the house where I'm boarding. But not the diary. That's gone—stolen."

Nancy admitted she had removed it, but someone had taken it from her. She now asked another question.

"Were you responsible for trying to harm Ned and me on various occasions?"

Gus shook his head vigorously. "Tuesday I followed you in a car to see where you lived. But I lost the trail in a parking lot in River Heights. I thought it would be better if you stopped snooping around here. I overheard a lot while I was in the house, and decided to attack Ned so he'd make you stay away from here. I sent him a note and then tried to knock him out in the school corridor. That's all I ever did."

By this time the three had reached the second floor. Bess and Dave came running forward, astounded.

"You caught the tapper?" Bess cried out. "It was the one you suspected, Nancy!"

Gus replied, "Yes, I'm the one who was doing the tapping. I took off my shoes and used the heels. But sometimes I used a hammer."

The group entered Miss Carter's room. After she had been told what had occurred in the attic, Gus went on with his story.

"As I told you, my parents went on a long trip and left me with two guardians, a couple named Gardner. They were pretty cruel—locked me in the secret room which they made from a storage area. Years ago you could only open the panel from the outside. But I fixed that lately.

"At the time my guardians kept me there, they

had an old man as kind of a guard whenever they went out. He used to fall asleep frequently and leave the panel open a little. Then I would sneak out and grab things which were my grandmother's. For a while I hid them in the secret room. There's a closet back of the bookcase, which moves. That's where I hid myself sometimes and why I set the mousetrap so nobody could find out the way to swing open the bookcase.

"I also made openings in wooden panels around the house and in the ceiling of the basement to hide my things in. After four years I forgot where they were and tapped trying to find them. By the way, the kitchen door to the basement was never locked until you girls came here. You made it hard for me to get around."

As Gus paused, Nancy asked Bess if she would go and get George and Burt. As soon as they arrived, the confession was resumed.

"Tell me," said Nancy, "when you had a chance to roam around the house and secrete various objects, why didn't you run away?"

Gus smiled. "I guess I was greedy. In any case I felt that what was rightfully mine I should hide while I could. I planned that as soon as I had found everything, I would gather them together and then go."

Gus went on to say that the plan had been interrupted when his parents suddenly took him off to the Beverly. He had waited nearly four years to get away from there.

"When I finally did, I came here to Berryville expecting to find my parents. To my surprise they had sold the house and vanished. Do you know anything about them?" he asked.

There was silence for a few moments, then Miss Carter spoke up. "Your parents passed away some time ago. Their estate was left in charge of a man named W. F. Bunce."

Gus lowered his eyes for a few moments as if in respect. "I'm sorry I was such a problem to them." Then he added, "I never heard of W. F. Bunce."

"By any chance did you knock out the man next door in the driveway Thursday night?"

Gus looked sheepish. "Yes, I did. I thought he might have seen me climbing down the wall. Besides, he was sneaking out of this house."

"Sneaking out of here!" Nancy repeated.

She had wondered why Bunce had never reported the attack to the police. Was it because he had recognized Gus and didn't dare go to the authorities? Or was it because he had illegally entered Miss Carter's house? It could even have been a contributing factor in his hasty exit from Berryville!

Nancy said to Gus, "We understand that your parents left a good bit of money in trust for you."

"What!" Gus exclaimed.

"Mr. Bunce was both the executor and administrator. He was supposed to send money to the Beverly to cover your expenses there, the way your father had, but we understand he never did. Dr. Jones was unaware your parents had died."

Nancy revealed all their suspicions about the couple who had been living next to Miss Carter and had moved out suddenly.

"Mr. Bunce had an automobile which was registered in your name."

"Why, the old cheat!" Gus cried out. "I haven't owned a car in years. I rent the ones I use now. Where can I find this man?"

Nancy smiled. "We're looking for him ourselves. We suspect he may know something about the theft of several of Miss Carter's valuable cats."

Gus looked at the floor. "Which one of you was tapping to me in Morse code?"

"I was," Nancy answered.

"It was very good." Gus chuckled. "Did you understand what I tapped back?"

It was Nancy's turn to grin. "You dared me to catch you. Well, I did!"

"I suppose," said Gus, "that this is the end of the line for me. My tapping heels helped to catch me. It seemed like fun at the time. Now, no doubt, I'm wanted by the police for breaking in here and burglarizing this place."

"I'm afraid so," the young sleuth replied. "Also, the police will want to know about the car you rented to follow me to River Heights. It had stolen license plates."

"I didn't know that," he declared.

At a nod from Nancy, Ned went to telephone headquarters.

Gus continued, "I think I'm all through running away."

Nancy hoped so. Perhaps, with a steady income, which he could earn from his knowledge of Morse code, Gus would act more mature. If Bunce had not spent all the money in the estate, there might be a good portion left for the rightful heir.

In a short time Detective Keely arrived. He was pleased that the tapper had been caught. Gus went willingly with him and another police officer.

After they had gone, Burt said, "This sure was an exciting evening. But now I guess it will have to come to an end. How about it, fellows?"

Reluctantly Ned and Dave agreed. Emerson College was a good many miles away and all three boys had early-morning classes.

"Let us know about any new developments," Ned requested. He chuckled as he added, "I sure enjoyed tackling Gus Woonton. Stopping a man on a football field is cool, but it can't compare with getting the better of a housebreaker!"

Bess spoke up. "Would you do me a big favor and take me home? River Heights is on your way."

"Sure thing," he answered.

George said she would like to go too. "Bess and I can come back tomorrow morning and bring Mrs. Bealing. Nancy, would you mind terribly staying here alone?"

"Of course not, especially since our mystery tapper has been caught."

Left alone with Miss Carter, Nancy brought a tray with hot cocoa and a few cookies for the actress and herself. While sipping their midnight beverage, the two talked about the mystery and hoped that Fred Bunce would be caught soon.

Presently Nancy kissed the actress good night and went to her own room. There was not a sound in the house nor outside, yet Nancy could not go to sleep. A sudden thought came to her. The secret trap door in the attic had not been closed.

"I'll go up and shut it," she said to herself.

Taking her flashlight, she went to the third floor. As Nancy neared the opened trap door, she became curious to know what lay below.

"Which part of the kitchen had the sealed-off stairway opened into?" she wondered. "Probably back of the cabinets."

Although Nancy went all the way to the bottom, she found nothing unusual except a box of sandwiches which Gus apparently had left there.

She turned back and came up. Just as she reached the top, a man's hand suddenly knocked her flashlight down and someone else clapped a hand over her mouth!

Nancy struggled, but was no match for her two strong opponents. She was bound and gagged, then made to slide down the steps. The trap door was closed and a heavy piece of furniture pulled across it.

CHAPTER XX

Amusing Confession

THE attack on Nancy had been so stealthy and unexpected she had not had a chance to see the faces of her assailants. She was sure there had been two men.

"Who could they have been?" she thought, puzzled. "Anyway, neither of them was Gus Woonton. So I have other enemies—possibly even Mr. Bunce!"

Suddenly a frightening idea came into her mind. Had the men harmed defenseless Miss Carter?

"Oh, I hope not." Nancy almost sobbed. "I must get out of this prison."

Nancy worked at the gag in her mouth and the bonds around her wrists and ankles but could not budge them. She was about halfway down the stairway. By lying on her back, and using her elbows and feet to propel herself, she managed to inch her way up to the door.

"I'd better not try standing, I might lose my balance," she decided.

Carefully Nancy switched herself around. Now, with her head pointed downward, she tapped her heels loudly on the attic door. She waited a minute, then tapped again. Silence.

"Oh, why did I let myself get into such a fix!" Nancy chided herself. "But I musn't give up."

The strong movement of her feet helped to loosen the bonds on them a bit. Hopefully she banged on the door again, but in vain.

"It's no use," she thought. "Even if Miss Carter wasn't injured by those men, she couldn't possibly get up here to help me. But when she finds I'm not in bed and hears the noise up here, maybe, just maybe, she'll telephone the police or drag herself up the stairs by using the railing."

Nancy continued to tap violently on the door. By this time she was nearly exhausted and had to rest a moment before doing anything more.

Then suddenly she heard voices. They were indistinct, but Nancy was sure they were not men's. With all the strength she had left she tapped again furiously.

In a moment she heard running footsteps on the attic stairway.

A voice came to her distinctly. "I don't see anyone," Bess Marvin called.

Nancy's heart leaped with relief. She hit the trap door again. Within seconds the heavy piece of furniture had been moved away. The trap door was lifted up. Five faces stared down at her in disbelief. Bess, George, Ned, Burt, and Dave stood there.

Nancy was quickly lifted into the attic and the gag and bonds removed. Bess flung both arms around her friend, completely blocking off any affectionate hugs the others might have wished to give her.

George's face showed anger. "Who did this to you?" she demanded.

"Two men came up behind me while I was investigating this stairway."

"I'll call the police," Ned said, but Burt said, "You stay with Nancy. I'll do it."

Ned could see that Nancy was pretty shaken. He swooped her up and carried the exhausted girl to the second floor.

As they passed Miss Carter's door the young people heard her call out, "What's going on? Come in and tell me."

Nancy was relieved that the woman had not been harmed. Bess opened the door and the actress gave a little scream.

"Oh, what has happened to Nancy?"

"I'll be all right, really I will," Nancy insisted.

Ned carried her to the couch and sat down beside her. Holding one of her hands, he said, "It would help if you could tell us the story, but if you don't feel up to it, we can wait."

"My mouth is dreadfully dry from that gag," Nancy said. "I'd appreciate a glass of water."

When she was ready to tell her story, the first thing she said was, "Did one of you have a hunch that I was in trouble?"

George replied, "Oh, you mean what brought us back here? Bess left her handbag."

Bess smiled. "Thank goodness I did."

Nancy said, "I suppose those two men aren't in the house any longer, but it wouldn't hurt to search."

At once the three boys went off and made a complete investigation. Just as they were reporting to the others that the intruders were gone, the telephone rang. Ned answered it.

"Police headquarters calling," a voice said. "Who is this?"

Ned identified himself and said he was a friend of Nancy Drew.

"This is Captain Healey," the officer told him. "Fred Bunce is under arrest here with a pal of his. We caught them running out of Miss Carter's driveway.

"I didn't call you until we had a complete confession. Bunce talked William Woonton into making him sole executor and administrator of the estate. He has stolen a good deal of it, but declares there's plenty left for Gus."

"I'm glad to hear that," said Ned. "Officer, if you can wait a moment, I think Nancy Drew should come to the phone and talk to you. She may have some questions."

Quickly Ned went upstairs and relayed the message. Nancy picked up the extension in Miss Carter's room and identified herself.

"I'm so happy you caught Bunce. Is his companion the person who stole the cats?"

"That's right," Captain Healey replied. "He's the one you saw sneaking away across the Bunces's yard. He disappeared into his friend's house until the search for him was over."

Healey also said that Bunce had kept a close watch on Gus even inside the house. In this way he had learned of the secret room and the diary, which he planned to steal, but Nancy had taken it before he had a chance. He had sent the cat thief to her house to get it. Bunce had also used this man to go to his home after the couple had left to pick up articles. Nancy, Bess, and George had nearly caught him.

"Bunce suspected that Gus was hunting for hidden treasures and planned to get the secrets out of you, Miss Drew. But the arrival of your boy friend upset that scheme."

"How did he find Gus?" Nancy said.

"From things Gus's parents said, Bunce figured that if Gus ever escaped from the Beverly he might come to his old home."

Nancy asked if Bunce and his companion were responsible for various attempts to harm her.

They included putting the bomb under her car, knocking over the scenery on the stage, starting the fire under the school stage and imprisoning her in the secret stairway.

"They did those things to you?" the officer cried out. "Hold the phone a minute."

There was a very long minute before he came back to say the men had confessed.

"They have a lot to answer for," he said. "And now perhaps you could answer a question for me. Do you know who hit Bunce over the head and knocked him out?"

"It was Gus Woonton. When Gus was climbing down from one of his nightly trips, he saw Bunce sneaking out of the Carter house. Gus hit him over the head to scare Bunce from entering again."

"You mean Bunce had a key to Miss Carter's house?"

"Yes, and to the garage also. Even after the locks were changed, he apparently made wax impressions and got a new set of keys."

The officer chuckled. "Tomorrow morning Bunce and Gus will meet here. It will be an interesting introduction."

Captain Healey promised to let Nancy know of any further developments. He said good-by and hung up.

Suddenly it occurred to Nancy that there was one part of the mystery which had not yet been solved. She said to the others in the room, "When I was questioning Gus Woonton about the tapping, he declared that he had never done any of it on the second floor, yet I distinctly heard tapping there last night."

Suddenly Miss Carter gave one of her trilly little laughs. She reached over and pulled open the drawer in a night table beside her bed. From it she took out a pair of tap shoes.

"I danced in these on the stage years ago," she said. "Sometimes, for memory's sake, I like to play with them."

She inserted her hands into the toes, raised her arms over her head, and began to tap on the headboard of her bed.

Nancy and her friends burst into laughter. The actress's eyes sparkled as the audience began to clap. Finally she stopped and put her arms down.

"I'm sorry I became part of that mystery, Nancy. I never dreamed that anyone could hear me tapping."

The young detective got up from the couch and went to hug Miss Carter. "I'm glad you have fun with your tap shoes. Now that the secret is out, I guess the whole mystery really is solved."

The other young people had risen too. They said good night for a second time and left for River Heights.

The following day Bess and George brought Mrs. Bealing back. She declared that now she did not mind staying alone with Miss Carter. Even the chore of taking care of the cats would not seem so hard. In a little while the three girls said good-by to the two women and went out to their cars.

"I just can't wait to see the play," Bess called to Nancy. "It's day after tomorrow, isn't it?"

On the night of the show, there were two whole rows of people who had come to see Nancy perform. Mr. Drew and Hannah Gruen were among them, as well as the Marvins and the Faynes and the three boys.

As a surprise Toby Simpson had brought Miss Carter and Mrs. Bealing. When Nancy came out for her first number, she was so surprised to see them that she almost forgot one of her lines.

The play went smoothly and was loudly applauded. When it came time for Nancy's final number, she decided to make it her best. She received a tremendous ovation and had to come back for an encore.

Suddenly Nancy decided to try something new. She waved to the orchestra leader not to play the music again. Then she began to tap.

The audience listened attentively, puzzled looks on their faces. Many of them caught on to the fact that the tapping sounded like a coded message but they could not decipher it.

Actually she was tapping out, "If anyone can

read this, tell me if you have a mystery for me to solve."

When she stopped dancing, and before anyone had a chance to clap, a young soldier stood up and waved an arm.

"You were tapping in code and I know what you said." He repeated her question. "I have one. It's *The Mystery of the Brass-Bound Trunk.*"

Her eyes twinkling, Nancy tapped back in code, "I'll take your case. Come backstage and tell me more about it after the show."

Nancy now motioned to the orchestra leader and she did an encore to the last part of her regular number. The audience laughed and began to whisper, wondering what she had said to the young soldier.

As Nancy came to a whirlwind finale, there was tremendous applause and whistles from her listeners. Then a "Yea, Nancy Drew!"

A STITCH IN TIME
SAVES NINE
Lions
and
Tigers